ADVENTURES OF THE ARGONAUTS

ADVENTURES OF THE ARGONAUTS

Retold by

W. H. D. ROUSE

With illustrations by KUPFER-SACHS

CHAPEL-EN-LE-FRITH
NIGEL GOURLAY, ASHWORTH HOUSE

First Edition . . . **1940**
Reprinted . . . 2020

CONTENTS

These names may be spoken like English words, and the accent in each name will help. The long mark ‾ means that a vowel takes twice as long to speak as a short one, like "fool" long, "full" short.

Properly c is always sounded as k; ch as kh, or ch in *loch*; a, e, i, o, u, as in Italian, *i.e.*:

a as in fäther, or hăt	o as in lōne, or pŏt
e ,, ,, (French) crême, or pĕt	u ,, ,, fool, or fŭll
i ,, ,, heel, or ill	eu ,, ,, yew

The mark ∧ in the text, as Achîllês, means it is not a silent vowel, but forms a syllable.

A-bў-dos	Cas-san-drā	Hes-pe'-ri-des	Per-co-lĕ
A-che-lŏi-os	Cas'-tor	Hip-po'-li-tĕ	Pei-ri'-tho-os
A'-che-rŏn	Cer'-be-ros	Hy-lās	Per-se-pho-nei'-a
A-che-rū-si-an	Cer-cŏ'-pes	Hyp-si'-py-lĕ	Pe'-lops
A-chil'-lēs	Cir'-cĕ	I'-dās	Phā-sis
Ad-mē'-tos	Ci-thai'-rŏn	Id'-mŏn	Phai-a'-ci-an
Ae-gī'-na	Cly'-ti-os	I-nŏ	Pha'-e-thŏn
A-gau'-ĕ	Col'-chis	I-o-lā-os	Phe'-rĕs
Aī'-a-cos	Cor-cў-ra	I-ŏl'-cos	Phī'-neus
Ai-dī'-ā	Chal'-ci-o-pē	I-phi-clĕs	Pho'-los
Ai'-ās (Ajax)	Cha-ly'-be-ans	I'-ris	Phrix'-os
Ai-ĕ'-tās	Cha-ryb'-des	Jā'-sŏn	Phron'-tis
Ai'-o-los	Cher'-so-nĕse	Lĕ-da	Pi-ty-ei'-a
Ai'-sŏn	Chei'-rŏn	Lĕm'-nos	Pol'-lux
Ai-tha'-li-dēs	Cre'-ŏn	Ler'-noi	Po-ly-deu'-cĕs
Al-ci'-no-os	Crĕ'-theus	Ly'-cos	Po-ly-phe'-mos
Alc-mē-nĕ	Cū-rĕ'-ti-an	Lyn'-ceus	Po-lyx'-ŏ
Al'-cy-o-neus	Cy-a'-ne-an	Mar-pĕs'-sa	Po-sei'-dŏn
Al-thai'-ā	Cy-rĕ-nē	Mĕ-dei'-a	Pro-mē'-theus
A'-ma-zŏn	Cў-zi-cos	Me'-ga-rā	Pro-pon'-tis
Am-bro'-si-a	Dĕ-i-a-nei'-ra	Mei-la'-ni-ŏn	Pў-tha'-go-rās
Am-phi-a-rā'-os	Del'-phĕ	Me-le-ag'-ros	Rha-da-man'-thys
Am'-phi-da-mās	Dĕ-mē'-tĕr	Me-lam'-pūs	Rhī-pai'-an
Am-phi'-try-ŏn	Di-o-mē'-dĕs	Me'-li-tĕ	Rho'-da-nos
Am-phi-trī'-tĕ	Di-o-nў-sos	Me-noi'-ti-os	Scyl'-la
A-my-thā'-ŏn	Dŏ-dŏ'-na	Mĕ-thym'-na	Se-me-lĕ
An-cai'-os	Ē-chei'-ŏn	Mī'-nŏs	Sī'-rĕn
A-phro-dī'-tĕ	Ē-ly'-si-an	Mī'-nŏ-taur	Sī'-sy-phos
Ap-syr'-tos	Ē-ri'-da-nos	Mop'-sos	Stym-phā-los
A'-rēs (Mars)	E-ri-phў'-lĕ	My-cĕ-nai	Syr'-tis
Ar'-gŏ	Eu-phĕ'-mos	Myr'-mi-don	Tai'-na-ron
Ar'-gos	Eu-ry'-di-cĕ	Mў'-si-ā	Ta'-lŏs
A-ri-ad'-nē	Eu-ry'-py-los	Ne'-me'-a	Tan'-ta-los
Ar'-te-mis	Eu-ry'-stheus	Ne'-phe-lĕ	Tar'-ta-ros
A-ta-lan'-ta	Eu'-ry-tos	Nĕs'-sos	Tei-re'-si-ās
A'-tha-mās	Ga-ny-mē'-dĕs	Nes'-tŏr	Te'-la-mŏn
A-thē'-na	Gĕ'-ry-o-nĕs	Ni'-sy-ros	The'-mis
A'-thŏs	Glau'-cos	O-ī'-leus	Thĕ'-rā
Au-ge'-ās	Hā'-dĕs	Oi'-neus	Ther-mŏ'-dŏn
Au-to'-no-ĕ	Ha'-lys	Om'-pha-lĕ	Thĕ'-seus
Bat'-tos	Hĕ'-bĕ	Or'-pheus	The'-tis
Be-brў-ci-an	He'-ca-tĕ	Pa'-ga-sai	Tī'-ryns
Bi-thў-ni-an	Hĕ'-li-os	Pal-lĕ'-nĕ	Tī'-phys
Bo'-re-ās	Hel'-lĕ	Pa'-tro-clos	Tī'-ty-ās
Bri-a'-re-ŏs	Hĕ-phais'-tos	Pe-las'-gi-an	Tri-nac'-ri-an
Cad'-mos	Hĕ'-rā	Pĕ'-leus	Trī-tŏ'-ni-an
Ca'-la-is	Hĕ'-ra-clĕs	Pe'-li-ās	Tў-phŏn
Ca'-ly-dŏn	Her'-cu-lĕs	Pĕ'-li-on	Zā'-tās
Ca-lyp'-sŏ	Her'-mĕs	Pe-ri-cly'-me-nos	Zeus

I

HOW THE STORY BEGAN

THIS is rather a long story, and you cannot understand it unless you know how it began. Indeed, the beginning is almost the strangest part of it. Just imagine a crowd of people in an old Greek city, all dressed in their best, King and Queen and grand people, priests in white robes trimmed with gold, incense and singing, and a long procession marching slowly to the high temple, to make a sacrifice at their altar to their gods; and in the middle two victims being led along to be killed and offered on the altar. But the victims are—what do you think? A little boy and a little girl; and these were the son and daughter of the King, but not of this Queen, for their mother had left him and flown up into the Clouds— indeed, she was a Cloud, or in their language, Nephelê. The new Queen was Ino; she hated the old children, and loved her own, so she made a plot against the old ones, named Phrixos and Hellê, and managed to convince the people that the children ought to be sacrificed. Do you want to know how, and why? I can tell you all that, but if I tell you everything, you will never get to my story at all, so I had better go on.

Flying up into the clouds, with the sun shining on his golden fleece.

Well, here is the procession, and here are the priests leading the two children towards the altar, and ready to sacrifice them to the angry gods. The children are brought to the altar, the priests are ready with their knives, when what is this they see! Some one looks up to the sky, and sees a bright something coming down like a falling star: everyone looks up, and lo and behold, a huge Ram with a golden fleece flies down from the clouds to the ground—so mother Cloud had not been idle, you see. Down comes the Ram beside the children, and they take the hint: up jumps Phrixos upon the Ram's back, and he pulls up Hellê, and the Ram gives a jump, and before the astonished priests can do anything, he is flying up into the clouds, with the sun shining on his golden fleece.

He steers eastwards, and flies steadily along, and they sail across the bay, across the sea, until after a while they arrive over the great river which flows out of the Black Sea. And there Hellê becomes dizzy, and all of a sudden she lets go of the golden fleece, and topples over and drops in the sea. There Hellê is drowned, and ever afterwards this part of the strait has been called Hellespont, or the sea of Hellê.

Phrixos could do nothing now, and the Ram went on, until he came to a great city on the east of the Black Sea, in the land of Colchis. There the King of Colchis lived, named Aietas, son of Helios the Sun; he received Phrixos, and gave him his daughter Chalciopê for a wife. Then he sacrificed the Ram, and hung up the golden fleece on a tree to be guarded by a great Dragon.

Phrixos and Hellê lived at a town in Thessaly, called Pagasai; and now we must turn to Iolcos, another Thessalian town. There the King was uncle to Phrixos, and when he died, his heir was his son, Aison; but the half-brother of Aison, named Pelias, seized the throne, and left Aison to live in a quiet way. However, Aison did not forget that he was the proper

King; and he did not trust Pelias at all.   So when his son Jason was born to him, it seemed prudent to get him out of the way.   The family pretended that the boy was dead, and filled the house with lamentation; but they wrapt up the baby in purple swaddling clothes (as befitted a royal child) and conveyed him to the mountains, and let no one into the secret except Night alone.   In the mountains lived one of those strange monsters, the Centaurs, half man and half horse; and this one, Cheiron, used to keep a sort of little public school for the heroes, with his wife and

Cheiron brought the boy up, showing him how to run and ride and shoot.

mother. Cheiron brought the boy up, showing him how to run and ride and shoot, and letting him kill what animals he could with his little bow and arrows, and his little spear, and teaching him all the herbs and flowers and trees, and the secrets of medicine, as well as good manners: for his great maxim was, honour Zeus first among the gods, and first among men, your father.

There Jason lived for twenty years, without offending his hosts in word or deed. His name means healer, and he was always one for gentle speech and justice, as you shall hear. He won the favour of the great goddess Hera too. For she used to travel about on earth, and test men to see what they were like; and she came once upon Jason on the bank of a river, in the shape of an ugly old hag; but when she asked him to help her, he did not laugh at her as an ugly old hag, but carried her across on his back. So Hera was always his friend.

But Pelias had a bad conscience; so he inquired of the oracle at Delphi, and there he was told "to beware of a man with only one understanding." This puzzled him, as it was meant to do—for how many understandings can a man have?

One day a young stranger came into the market-place, a fine handsome boy with long hair flowing over his shoulders, carrying a couple of spears, and dressed in close-fitting tunic and leggings, with a leopard-skin flung over all.

"Who on earth can this be?" said the people to

one another. "We never saw him before, and he is as handsome as some one in a fairy tale!"

The rumour came to Pelias in his palace, and he thought he had better see who it was, because as I told you his conscience was not easy.

"My car!" he called out to his men, "put in a pair of good mules, and look sharp." Then he rattled along the stony street, and what should he see in the market place but this fine young stranger, with only one shoe on his right foot, and the left foot bare.

"Ha!" thought Pelias to himself. "The man with one understanding! I understand now! So that was what the oracle meant." But he hid the fear in his heart, and called out rudely:

"Where do you come from, young stranger? Some old hag was your mother, I suppose, and your cradle was a ditch. I hate a liar, so tell me the truth."

The boy answered quietly and politely.

"You shall see, Sir, that Cheiron has taught me manners. I have lived in his cave for twenty years, and his kind wife and mother have brought me up; and all that time I have not spoken a rude word or done a rude thing. I come now to claim the ancient royalty of my father, which is his by inheritance from his grandfather Aiolos; but it has been usurped from him, as I hear, by one Pelias. When I was born, my father pretended that I was dead, and made a funeral here; but they gave me over to Cheiron to bring up.

"Now, my good people, tell me the way to my father's house; for I am no stranger, but Aison's son, come home to his own country. My name is Jason the Healer, at least the old Centaur called me so."

Pelias held his tongue, but the people showed him the way to his father's house, and his father saw him: tears fell from the old eyes, but there was joy in his heart when he saw the splendid boy, his own son. Aison's two brothers came as soon as they heard the news. Pheres from his country and Amythaon from his; Admetos and Melampus, two cousins of the lad, came also to welcome him. A fine feast was made; Jason entertained them for five days and five nights, with the best of good cheer, and friendly talk.

On the sixth day, he spoke to his kinsmen in serious mood, and told them all from beginning to end. Then they all rose and went from their house with him to the mansion of Pelias. They entered the hall, and stood there, while Jason spoke to Pelias gently and kindly, and built a foundation for a friendly understanding, something like this.

"Most honourable Sir, men's hearts are quicker to choose gain than justice, although they ought to think of to-morrow's hangover after the feast. But you and I, Sir, should school our passions, and so do that happiness may follow. The Fates who allot our portions hide their faces if kinsmen quarrel. We are kinsmen, we must never take sword and spear to divide our great inheritance. I yield to you flocks and herds and broad acres, all that you have taken from my father to increase your riches, and I grudge you nothing of that; but give me sceptre and throne, and the royal state which my father inherited from his father: let us agree in this, that there may be no quarrel between us."

Pelias answered quietly: "I will agree to that. But I am old, my hair grows white, and you are in the prime of your young life, so you can appease the wrath of the gods below. Phrixos bids us to lay his unquiet spirit. Go to the court of Aietas, and bring back the golden fleece of the Ram, which saved him once from the sea and from the wicked plot of his stepmother Ino. This is what a wonderful dream tells me. I have asked advice of the oracle at Delphi, and I am told to send a ship for it. Be so good as to undertake this task, and I swear I will grant you to be King and monarch here. I swear my solemn oath by Zeus our family god."

So they made their agreement, and parted. Jason then sent heralds to proclaim the coming voyage in all places. Quickly came three mighty sons of Zeus, one being son of Alcmenê, Heraclês, or Herculês as some called him, and two of Leda, Castor and Polydeucês or Pollux. Heraclês heard the summons when he was coming home after one of his Labours, and carried the famous boar on his shoulders. He dumped the boar down in the market place of Mycenæ, and set out at once, with young Hylas to carry his bow and arrows. Castor was the great horseman of Sparta, and Polydeucês was a boxer famous all over the world. They were brothers of Helen, and both born from one large egg. Another story, you see! Then came two tall men, sons of Poseidon Earth-shaker, springheel Euphemos, the quickest runner on earth—he could skim the surface of the sea by dipping the ends of his toes, while he kept his feet dry; and Periclymenos, who was very strong and could take on any shape he liked, in battle. Nor must I forget Orpheus the famous musician, who could charm rivers and rocks and make the trees dance to his music. Apollo sent him, and Hermes sent two sons, Echeion and Eurytos, Holdfast and Pullhard. Boreas the North Wind also sent two sons, Zatas and Calaïs, with purple wings quivering on their shoulders. Polyphemos[1] came too, one who had fought against the Centaurs in his young days, now old but brave as ever in battle. Menoitios also came, whose son Patroclos became so famous in the Trojan War, and Oïleus, the father of little Aias; Telamon, father of big Aias, and Peleus, father of Achilles. Another was Tiphys, the navigator and pilot; Idmon another, a wise prophet who knew the voices of birds, son of Apollo, who himself taught him the art of prophecy: he knew his own fate, but he came all the same. Ancaios came from Calydon: his grandfather did not want him to go, and hid his armour; but Ancaios wrapt a bearskin round him, and carried a huge two-edged battle-axe. Idas and Lynceus were a famous pair. The god Apollo was in love with a girl Marpessa, but Idas carried her off in a winged chariot. Then Apollo caught him, and the two lovers fought; but Zeus stopt the fight, and told Marpessa to choose. She chose Idas, and Apollo had to grin and bear it. And Lynceus had the sharpest sight of any man on

[1] Not the monster of the Odyssey, but a Lapith.

earth; indeed, he could even see what was under the earth. Both the brothers took part in the Calydonian Hunt, after the return of the voyagers. Another story! Meleagros came too, a young man, who later came to untimely death by his mother's hand: when he was born the Fates declared he would die when the brand then burning on the hearth should be burnt up; his mother put it out, and laid it in a chest, but later she became angry with him, and took it out and burnt it, so Meleagros died. This was after he had killed the Calydonian boar. These were not all, but they were chief of the Argonauts. There was one girl, Atalanta.

The goddess Athena herself taught Argos how to build the ship Argo, and she fitted in the stem an oak beam that she had brought from Dodona, a divine speaking beam from the speaking oak of Dodona.

When the ship was ready, and all the stores on board, a great crowd of people gathered to see the heroes set forth, the women raising their hands to heaven and praying to the gods for a safe return. Jason's father and mother were full of sorrow, now their boy was going on such a dangerous quest; but Jason full of confidence bade them take courage.

"My mother, your grief can do me no good. We have to endure what the gods send us, and now they all tell us to go. Be yourself a good omen to me, not a bad one!"

So he passed on to the beach, and the people gazed in admiration at his fine looks and bearing; the old Priestess of the city kissed his hand, but could not speak; and he left her there, as the young must leave the old. When Jason came down to the beach, he called all the heroes together, and said:

"Now choose your leader."

Heraclês rose, and said: "Do not choose me; I will not consent, and I forbid any other to stand up. Let Jason be our leader, as Jason has gathered us out of all the land."

All approved, and Jason said:

"If you entrust yourselves to me, let us now make sacrifice to Apollo, who has promised me a good voyage, and let us launch our ship into the sea."

There was a wide and deep trench leading from the ship to the sea; in this they laid rollers. The ship had been made ready, with the oars laid across, and projecting at the ends a foot or two; the heroes breasted these oars, on both sides, and pushed forward with chest and hand at once, Tiphys the helmsman calling aloud to give the time. The Argo glided down to the sea; the men leapt in, and fitted the oars to the tholepins. Then they did sacrifice on the shore, and Idmon the seer said:

"It is the will of heaven that you shall return in safety, with the Golden Fleece; but many trials await you in between. My lot is to die; I knew this even before, by the omens which I see, but I came to save my own honour."

They all came aboard, and Jason counted them to see they were all there; Mopsos the seer was glad to tell them that omens were good; old Cheiron was on the beach, he waded soon into the sea, waving a hand, and crying: "Good luck to you, and a safe return!"

His wife was beside him, nursing the little Achillês, and she held up the boy to say Good-bye to his father Peleus on board. Then Jason took a golden goblet of wine, and stood upon the poop, and offered his prayer to Zeus Thunderspear; he prayed also to the waves and currents of the sea, and the winds, and the watery paths, and day and night, to show a good heart to him and grant a safe return. A timely omen came from the clouds, an answering clap of thunder and bright flashes of lightning. The heroes fell easy all, for they had faith in those divine signs; but the seer told them to paddle on and have good hopes, with Tiphys at the helm.

Soon they left the harbour, and pulled in their oars: the mast was set up in the box, and fastened taut with stays, the yard was hauled up and the sail was let fall; a piping breeze filled the sail, and they ran past the headland. Orpheus touched his harp, and sang of Artemis who was lady of that shore; and the fish both great and small played along beside the ship. They ran past the Pelasgian cornlands and rocky Pelion, and the prong of Pallenê, with the dark mass of Mount Athos in front, and came after some days to the island of Lemnos.

There had been a quarrel in Lemnos, between the men and their wives, and the wives had killed their husbands and every man or boy they could find, but they were soon sorry. Hypsipylê alone, the queen, had spared her old father, but she only put him into a chest and set him afloat on the sea. The women left off spinning and weaving, and plowed the fields instead of the men. When they saw the Argo and its crew, they thought these were men from Thrace come to punish them; and they put on the men's armour, and ran down to the harbour in dismay.

The heroes had sent out their herald, Aithalidês, a son of Hermês, with the wand of Hermês in his hand. He was a wonderful man; for Hermês his father had given him a memory which never grew dim, not even later, when he entered the house of Hadês; and now his fate is to be sometimes under the earth, sometimes living among men, but always remembering the past. His soul afterwards entered into the body of Pythagoras the philosopher, and Pythagoras could remember his former lives. But now he spoke gently to Hypsipylê, and persuaded her to let them in. She called a meeting of the women of Lemnos, and said:

"My friends, these are not enemies; and I think we should let them have food and whatever they want, so long as they will keep without our walls."

Then her old nurse Polyxo rose, and said:

"My friends, it is all very well now, but what will it be when you are old, and there is no one to plow the fields? The oxen will not plow of themselves, and we have enemies on the mainland. My advice is, to let them come in."

They agreed, and sent for Jason. When he appeared, clad in a splendid mantle of purple dye, richly embroidered, with a spear in his hand, Hypsipylê fell in love with him at sight, and told him a false tale, for she was ashamed to tell the truth. She said that the men of Thrace had carried off their husbands, and begged him to bring his people in. They came in, and the women entertained them all, and received them into their houses, all but Heraclês and a few others who remained on board. Then their sailing was delayed from day to day, until Heraclês was tired of waiting.

"Look here, you men," he said, "we shall get neither good nor credit by staying here. Let us leave Jason to dally with his Hypsipylê, and return home ourselves."

So they made ready to go; and when it was known, all the women came buzzing about them like a swarm of bees, and Hypsipylê with them; and she cried:

"Go, and good fortune go with you! and I pray that you may bring back the Golden Fleece!"

Then they all embarked, and Argos loosed the hawsers, and by evening they were in the straits. They passed the Chersonese on the left, and Abydos and Percolê and Pityeia the Pinetown, and entered the Propontis, and lay to in the harbour of Cyzicos. The country thereabouts was inhabited by fierce giants who had six arms each, two on his shoulders and four below, but they did them no harm. The King gave them provisions, and they talked long together.

But when they sailed on the next day, they were driven into a neighbouring harbour where they lay to, and they were attacked by the monstrous creatures of the country. There was a battle, the heroes sailed out, and got back to Cyzicos without knowing it.

The people attacked them now, as strangers, and the King himself was killed.

They came next to Mysia, and the people received them kindly and supplied their needs, sheep and wine, wood and leaves to sleep on. Heraclês in pulling had broken his oar; so he went into the woods to get another. Seeing a tall fir tree, he thought that would do. He laid bow and quiver on the ground, and threw off his lion-skin, and seizing the tree with his hands, he pulled it up by the roots; for he was very strong. Meanwhile, Hylas his page with a bronze pail went in search of water. A nymph of the spring saw him, and loved him at sight; she laid her left arm over his neck and drew him down into the water. The boy cried out, and one of the men, Polyphemos, hearing his cry, ran to the rescue. On the way, he saw Heraclês, and said:

"Bad news for you! Hylas has gone for water, and robbers have attacked him, or wild beasts perhaps —I heard his cry for help!"

Heraclês threw down the fir tree, and ran to the rescue shouting.

But morning came, and he had not come back. Tiphys hurried all aboard, and set sail, and no one noticed that Heraclês was a-missing; but at last Telamon saw it, and made an outcry. Then Tiphys would have turned back, but there was a quarrel, and suddenly they saw rising out of the sea, the body of the sea-god Glaucos, who said to them:

"Why do you wish to take Heraclês on this quest, against the will of Zeus? For his fate is to do twelve great Labours first, and then to be raised to heaven; and Polyphemos is to found a city here in Mysia.   A divine nymph has made Hylas her husband, and those two have gone to seek him."

Then he sank down again into the sea, and the heroes went on.

II

THE BOXING MATCH

THE wind now brought them to the land of the Bebrycians, an arrogant nation: for their King had made a rule that if strangers came, they should not depart until they had faced him in the boxing-ring; and he had slain many in this way. He came down to the ship, and shouted out:

"Listen, you wanderers! I don't know who you are and I don't care, but you shall not go on until you have had a boxing-match with me. So choose your man, and bring him out, for I beat the world at boxing!"

This made them angry, but they had their man all ready—Polydeucês the Spartan Chicken. He stept out at once, and said:

"Here I am, quite ready to obey your majesty's rules."

They found a good place, and faced each other: on one side a monstrous savage, on the other side a fine young fellow, quick on his feet, and ready to put brain against brawn. The King's servant laid between them two pairs of gauntlets, made of thick straps of hide; meant to hurt, not to make the blow less, as our gloves are.

"Choose which you like," said the King, "and you shall see how nicely I can carve your face!"

So the Spartan Chicken stood up to the Bebrycian Bombardier. There was a great deal of moving about, to see which could get the sun at his back; then the Chicken did it, because as I told you, he was a springheel, and the other was too heavy to move well. So the Bombardier finds he has the sun in his face, and goes sparring forwards, but the Chicken got home on his chin: the Bombardier lost his temper at that, and forced the fighting, butting hard like a bull at a gate. But the Chicken dodged him and popped in a double left and right, and stopt him, till he stood dazed by the blows, and a copious flow of claret ensued. The other side cheered uproariously to see the state of his mug; his kisser was badly marked, and his jaws were barked, and both his goggles were closing up as his face began to swell. The Chicken followed up with a series of feints, till the other man was fairly puzzled, then delivered a spank on the middle of his snuff-box and took off all the japan. Down he went flat on his back in the leaves; but he was not out yet, he got up and a fierce battle followed, they punished each other with their knuckledusters, until the Bombardier went for his body and neck, but the indomitable Chicken landed some ugly ones and barked all his frontispiece. Then the Bombardier caught the Chicken's left with his left, and swung in a good 'un with his right, which would have done for him; but the Chicken ducked his knowledge-box and got in a right-hander on his

But the Chicken got home on his chin.

left listener, drawing the ruby, then he got home with his left on the potato-trap and clattered his ivories, and rang such a rattat on his physiog with both daddles that he was all in a mess, till he broke the man's jaw and left him down and out.

Then the Bebrycians picked up clubs and spears or anything that was handy, and ran on Polydeucês; but his men stood before him, sword in hand. Castor cleft one man's head as he ran at him; Polydeucês met one giant with a leap against his chest and threw him down in the dust with his foot; another he struck with his right hand above the left eyebrow, and tore the flesh away over his eyeball. The enemy did wound one or two, but killed none. Ancaios now caught up his black bearskin to defend himself, and wielded his battle-axe with his right; Jason and others charged with him, and scattered the proud Bebrycians like a flock of sheep. They dispersed everywhere as bees fly from a smoking hive, and in all the country-side they were met and killed by their enemies, who were glad of the chance.

The heroes dressed their wounds, and feasted in peace on the beach; the next day they filled the Argo with spoils and sailed down the Bosporos; and next day they came to the Bithynian land, near the mouth.

There old Phineus was King, an old unhappy man who had received from Apollo the gift of prophecy; he knew the will of Zeus, and what was going to happen, and he told it all to those who came to ask. But Zeus does not allow this; even Apollo must not tell all, but only part of the mind of Zeus: so Zeus made the old man blind, and he would not let him enjoy the gifts which people brought him for his prophecies. He sent upon him a flock of dangerous birds, the Harpies or Snatchers; and when Phineus used to set out a feast before him, the Harpies would swoop down, and snatch the food and drink from his lips, and leave him amid a horrid stench while they mocked his misery. They left him only a scrap or two, just enough to keep him alive and miserable, and flew away. But the old man heard the heroes come, and by his divine knowledge, he knew they were come to deliver him.

So he rose from his couch, like a lifeless dream, and bowed over his staff he crept out on his withered feet, feeling the walls; his limbs trembled for weakness, his skin was parched and caked with dirt, and the skin did no more than hold his old bones together. So he came down to meet them, and fell dizzy to the ground, and there they saw him.

When they had propt him up, he told them his unhappy story.

"Listen to me, noble sirs," he said, "if you are truly the men of Jason in the ship Argo, seeking for the Golden Fleece. I know you are; I thank thee, Lord Apollo, unhappy though I am; and you noble sirs, help me now and save me from this cruel fate, by the favour of Apollo and of Hera herself, who is your friend. The Fury has trampled upon my eyes, and I cannot see; worse than that, when I would eat the Harpies swoop down on me, and take my food away, swift as lightning, and what they leave has such a stench that no one can come near me. Only necessity compels me to eat it. But the sons of the North Wind are to save me; they are akin to me, for I married their sister Cassandra."

Then Zatas took his hand, and said:

"What a wretched man you are, Sir! Have you sinned against the gods? for we will not help you, unless you swear that we shall not lose the favour of heaven."

The old man said:

"Fear not that, my son. Let Apollo be my witness, who gave me this gift of prophecy, and may the gods of the underworld curse me if I lie; no wrath of heaven shall come upon you if you will help me."

So Zatas and Calaïs prepared a feast, the last which the Harpies were to have, and both stood near him to see them come. Scarcely had he touched the food, when down came the Harpies like flashes of lightning, and swooped with shrieks greedy for food; they devoured all and flew away, leaving behind them an intolerable stench. Zatas and Calaïs darted up into the air on their shimmering wings, and caught them, and grazed them with their finger-tips; and they would have torn them to pieces, but Iris came down from heaven and said to them:

"It is not lawful, you sons of the North Wind, to destroy the hounds of Zeus; but I will promise you they shall come no more near to Phineus." Then she swore an oath by the waters of Styx, the most awful

The Harpies swoop down on me, and take my food away, swift as lightning.

and solemn oath which the gods can take, that this should be so; the Harpies flew home to their den in Crete, and the two sons of the North Wind flew back to Jason.

Meanwhile the heroes washed the old man's body clean, and set forth another feast, a real feast now; and as they sat waiting for Zatas and Calaïs, the old man told them of the end of their voyage.

"Not everything is lawful for you to know," he said; "formerly I used to tell all, but it is the will of Zeus to tell men only a part, that they may still have something to do themselves.

"First of all, you will see the twin Cyanean rocks at the mouth of the strait. No one, I think, has ever passed between them yet. They are not rooted to the ground, but they float, and constantly clash together till the waters rise and beat on the shore. You must send on a dove in advance, and let her fly through; if she gets through safe, you will know that it is the will of Zeus that the Argo should get through safe; if not, you must not attempt it. If you do get through, keep the coast on your right hand, and sail on past many an island and many a headland, sail past the river Halys, and past the river Thermodon, and then past the country of the Amazons, those warlike women who fight like men, and live without men; they wear armour, and carry a half-moon buckler, and ride on horseback. Sail past the country of the Chalybeans, who spend hard lives in digging for iron, because their soil is rough and yields little. Then pass the Treehutmen, who dwell not on earth but high in the branches of trees, where they build their huts. Many another tribe and nation you shall pass, till at last you arrive at the place where the river Phasis falls into the sea. There you shall see walls and towers, and the wood where the Golden Fleece hangs, guarded by a dragon."

All were silent, full of foreboding at this long tale of dangers; and at last Jason said:

"And when we have reached our goal, how shall we find our way back?"

Phineus answered: "You will easily find a guide to the place, and a god will show you another way back, not the way you came. But to win your quest, you must ask the help of Aphroditê the goddess of love."

Then the two sons of the North Wind returned, and Zatas told how the Harpies had been driven away, and how Iris had forbidden them to kill the monsters.

Phineus was now at peace, being cared for by the country folk whose friend he was; and the heroes made ready to go. Euphemos caught a dove and brought it along with him.

By and by they came to the north of the strait, and heard the noise of the Crashing Rocks, and saw them dash together, and the huge wave rise up between them, and flow down the cliffs. They opened again, and Euphemos let his dove fly. Away she flew, straight between; she grew smaller until she was a speck in the sky, but as they crashed for the next time, Lynceus could see her still—for he had the keenest sight of all men on earth—she flew through, but the rocks caught a tail feather.

"She's through, men!" he cried, and Tiphys told them to row with might and main as the rocks parted again. They did row then, and got halfway through, when the sea rolled in to meet them, and twisted the Argo round and round, and drove it back on the rocks. They were all terrified, but now they could see another great wave rising up to flow in behind the stern. It curled above them, and seemed about to drown them all; but Tiphys with his skill kept her stern-on to meet it—the great billow rolled under them and carried them out, the rocks crashed together and just caught her stern-ornament, and she was through. Then with a terrific sound the two rocks crashed together for the last time, and became one; they were rooted firmly below the water, and never moved again.

Now all were cheerful and full of courage, and they passed on their way. All day long they rowed, as easily as a team draws the plow through fat land. They put in at a desert island, and built an altar of sacrifice to Apollo, and danced and sang the song of the Healer; there they spent the night.

Next day they ran in by the Acherusian headland, which looks on the Bithynian Sea. There on the cliff is a cave of Hadês, from which comes ever an icy wind; and here rolls down Acheron, the river of Pain. They were welcomed by Lycos the King, who was an enemy of the Bebrycians; and Jason told them his wonderful story. When he heard how Heraclês had been left behind, Lycos said:

"I remember him. When I was a young man, he

came on foot out of Asia, bringing the girdle of the Amazon Hippolytê, which was given him as her sister's ransom. He boxed with the mighty Titias, and killed him, and brought the neighbouring tribes to be part of my father's realm; but since Heraclês went away, the Bebrycians have been encroaching upon our land, and now you have killed their King and we have beaten them off."

At this place, however, Idmon met his death; for he was attacked by a wild boar. They killed the boar, but Idmon died in the arms of his comrades. Tiphys the helmsman also died; he fell sick, and they could not save him. But a second Ancaios, a son of Poseidon, offered to take his place, for he also was one who had knowledge of ships; and there were others ready.

With a favourable wind, they passed by the land of the Amazons, while those formidable women were gathering to attack them; and passed the land of the Treehutmen, unhappy savage creatures—and unhappy is their King! He sits in the largest hut, and dispenses judgments; but if ever he makes a mistake, they shut him up in his hut and starve him all that day.

By and by they came to the island of Arês, which was haunted by the birds of Arês. These terrible birds had brazen feathers; they came from the Lake of Stymphalos, and Heraclês drove them away, for he could not kill such a swarm; and now they nested and lived in the Isle of Arês. One of them flew over the ship, and dropt a feather, which fell on the left shoulder of Oïleus as he rowed, and pierced him like an arrow. As his neighbour pulled out the feather, another bird flew over the ship; but Clytios saw it, and shot an arrow at it—so it turned over and fell close to the ship.

"Look there," said Amphidamas. "Arrows are of no use against these birds, and we shall never be able to land. Not even Heraclês could kill them with his arrows; but he showed us what to do—I saw it myself. He shook a bronze rattle and made a great noise, and they all flew away in fear. Let us take a lesson from Heraclês. Half of us row, half stand round the ship in armour, with shields and spears, and rattle the spears on the shields, and shout, and frighten them away!"

They did so; and when they came near the island, they made such a din, that the birds discharged a volley of feathers, and flew across to the mainland.

The heroes had been told to land here, but not why; but when they landed, they found out why. For there they found the four sons of Phrixos, who had been on their way home to claim their inheritance, when they were wrecked and washed up on this island.

"Who are you?" asked Jason; and Argos replied:

"No doubt you have heard of Phrixos, who came from Hellas on the Ram with the Golden Fleece. He married the King's daughter Chalciopê; we are their sons, and when he died, he told us to return to claim the possessions of Athamas."

"Well," said Jason, "then we are kinsmen;

Athamas and my grandfather Cretheus were brothers; and we are sailing to Colchis ourselves." Then he gave them dry clothes, and all they wanted.

"You may come with us," he said, "we want that same Golden Fleece!" This made them afraid. Argos said:

"King Aietas is a determined man, and that is no easy task." But Peleus said:

"Don't be afraid. He will give us the fleece for friendship's sake; and if he does not, we are strong enough to take it."

They sailed on together; and they saw the cliff where Prometheus was fettered, and heard his cry as the cruel eagle tore his liver. They saw the eagle soaring high in the sky, and at night they reached the river Phasis and the Colchian land. There they lay to for the night.

III

THE ARROW OF CUPID

You remember the old prophet's words, that to win
their quest they must ask the aid of the Goddess of
Love. They did not know what this meant, perhaps, but their friends in heaven knew, Hera and
Athena, and these two, as they saw the Argonauts
hiding in the thick reed-beds, began to think what
they had better do. They thought for a long time,
and then Hera said:

"I know what. We had better go to Aphroditê,
and beg her to tell her little boy Cupid to shoot an
arrow at Medeia the daughter of King Aietas, and
make her fall in love with Jason. She is a famous
witch, you know, and she can help."

Aphroditê, perhaps you know and perhaps you
have forgotten, was the wife of old Hephaistos. I
could tell you good stories about him, but if I do,
what will become of Jason? At least I can tell you
he was the great master of arts and crafts; he was
lame from an accident, and black and ugly, so that
the pair were like Beauty and the Beast. He was
blacksmith and goldsmith and architect in heaven.
He had built a fine house in Cyprus for Aphroditê,
and there they found her—for old Crookshank was

at the forge, and she was sitting on a chair, facing the door, and combing her long hair with a golden comb over her white shoulders.

"Come in, my dears!" she cried when she saw them, and jumped up from her seat, gathering her long bunches of hair up in her hands. Then she found seats for them, and sat down again and said:

"What brings you here? You don't often visit my humble home!"

Hera said: "Don't make fun of us, my dear, we are in a fix, and you must help us out. My friend Jason has brought the ship Argo to Colchis, with a magnificent crew of all the great heroes of Hellas, to get the Golden Fleece, and I am sure King Aietas won't give it up if he can help it. Jason is a friend of mine; he has fine manners; and when I met him in the shape of an ugly old hag, to see what he would do, he did not laugh at the old hag as rude young people do, but caught me up on his shoulders and carried me across the river, as I asked him. You can help me now; you know Pelias ought to be punished for the way he treated Jason and his father."

Aphroditê said: "You may count on me, if I can do anything." Hera said:

"We don't want war and violence. Just tell your boy to shoot an arrow at Medeia, the King's daughter. She can help him, you know, because she is a witch; and if she will, he will get that fleece easily enough."

"My dears, you don't know that boy! He will listen to you rather than me. He may be a bit ashamed to be rude to you, but he thinks nothing of me—just does what he likes, and laughs. He says: if I won't leave him alone, he'll make me sorry for it. I vow I'll break his bow and arrows, nasty whistling things, and he shall see me do it!'"

The other two smiled at each other, but Aphroditê saw it, and cried:

"You just laugh at my troubles! I ought to say nothing about them; I know them too well, that's enough. Well then, since you ask me, I'll try to coax him, and see what happens."

Hera took her hand and stroked it, smiling, and said:

"Thank you, my dear, just try; don't be angry, coax him, and I'm sure he will be a good boy."

So they went home, and she hurried up the hill to look for her boy. She found him in the orchard, playing for golden dice with Ganymedês his little chum. Cupid had got most of the dice already, and stood holding them fast in his left hand against his chest; the other sat crouched on the ground, with two dice left, which he threw one after the other, and lost them too: Cupid picked them up, and Ganymedês went off with empty hands, and Cupid only laughed at him. He did not see his mother until she came up and laid a hand on his lips, and said:

"Why do you laugh at him, you unutterable rogue? Have you cheated the poor innocent out of his dice? Come now, be a good boy and do something for me; and I will give you a beautiful toy. It belonged to Zeus himself once, when he was a little child in that Cretan cave. A ball! Crookshank himself couldn't make a better one. Gold rings all round, double seams round each, and you can't see the stitches! Throw it up, and it leaves a fairy track in the air like a falling star! All I ask is for you to shoot an arrow at Medeia, and make her fall in love with Jason. Be quick, now, and mother will be pleased."

Cupid threw down all the golden dice on the ground, and caught his mother's dress with a hand each side, and said:

"Now! Now, please!"

But she kissed him, and said smiling:

"I promise you, I won't deceive you, but you must shoot her first."

He picked up his dice, and threw them into her lap, and picked up bow and quiver which were leaning against a tree. Then he flew up into the air, and sailed over the earth with its mountains and cities and farms, on his way to Colchis.

Meanwhile the heroes were in council among the reeds, and Jason said to them:

"My friends, this is my advice. You stay here, and I will visit the King's palace, and the sons of Phrixos shall go with me and two others. First I will try gentle words, which often do what force cannot do. He entertained Phrixos, you know, and all men owe respect to the stranger."

The others agreed to this, and they set out. As they passed along the plain, they were surprised to see bundles hanging in all the trees, and still more surprised to find that these were the dead bodies of men. The reason is, that the Colchians think both fire and earth are holy, and so they will not bury their dead nor burn them, but they wrap them in oxhides and hang them up in the trees.

They soon came to the city and the King's palace, and a wonderful place it was. The King's father, you may remember, was Helios the Sun himself; the King's sister was Circê, the terrible witch who turned men into pigs—another story there, you see, which I have no time to tell now. His wife was a daughter of Ocean; so Aietas was a great man, and Crookshank Hephaistos had built him a palace, with a fine garden full of vines, and in it he made four fountains ever-flowing—one ran milk, one wine, one oil, and one water, warm at the setting of the Pleiades, but it turned cold at their rising. He made him also bulls with brazen feet and brazen mouths, which breathed fire; and a plow of adamant. There was an inner court, with a covered walk each side open to the air, and lofty buildings all round; one for the King and Queen, one for his son Apsyrtos, one for his two daughters, Chalciopê and Medeia, and one for the women in waiting. Medeia was priestess of the dark goddess Hecatê, but on this day she was at home, and seeing the strangers, she called Chalciopê, who greeted her four sons with joy—she had been the wife of Phrixos, you remember: she called out—

"So you were not to go far from your mother! Why should you go to that city, whatever it was, to get the wealth of Athamas, and leave me alone in my sorrow?"

Last of all, the King and Queen came out, and a crowd filled the courtyard. And while they were busy gazing and gossiping, or getting ready for dinner, lo and behold here came Cupid, flying through the air like a little gadfly, and nobody noticed him. He dropt down quietly in the porch and looked sharply round; gliding close beside Jason, he laid an arrow-notch on the cord, and pulled, and shot Medeia—then with a laugh he flashed out of the hall.

But the arrow went straight and buried itself deep in Medeia's heart. It burnt like fire, and she could not speak one word—just stood there dazed, and gazed at Jason; all memory left her, and her soul melted with sweet pain. Love burnt her heart like a crackling fire of dry twigs; her cheeks were now red, now pale, and she knew nothing but that Jason was there.

The banquet was laid, the company ate and drank, and King Aietas spoke.

"Young men," he said, "sons of Phrixos and my daughter, why have you come back? I told you what a long journey it was, I told you all the dangers you must meet in your voyage to the west, but what is the use of words? Tell me what happened, and who these strangers are." Argos replied:

"Our ship was wrecked, Sir, on the isle of Arês, but some god must have helped us: his brazen birds were not there, but we met these strange men, who saved us and cared for us, and brought us here. For Colchis was their goal: and they were glad when they heard the name of Phrixos, and your name. They say the gods are angry, and their curse will not fail until the Fleece comes back to Hellas. This is a wonderful ship Argo, which they have, proof against storm and wind, not like our Colchian Hoy which is wrecked by the first gale; she blows with any wind, and rows against any wind; and her crew are the noblest heroes of Hellas. But he comes not to use force; he is ready to pay the price of your gift; he will conquer your enemies for you. Jason is the leader of this company, and he is of our kin; for he is grandson of Cretheus, and Phrixos was the son of Athamas, the brother of Cretheus. Here is Augeias, the son of Helios your father; here is Telamon, whose father's father is Zeus; and all his comrades are sons or grandsons of the immortal gods."

But the King was furious. He thought this young man had brought them all in a plot against himself, and he said:

"Get you gone, you traitors! You want to seize my throne and sceptre, that's why you have come! If you had not eaten at my table, I would have torn out your tongues and cut off your hands, and left you only feet to go away with!"

Telamon would have spoken, in anger too; but Jason checked him, and said:

"Bear with us, your Majesty, we have no such desire. Who would dare to cross the wide sea only to rob a stranger? No! the command of a presumptuous King sent me. Grant us a favour, and we will make a good return; we will fight against your enemies for you, or anything else you wish."

So Jason, as always, used gentle words; and the King was silent awhile, as he considered what was best. At last he said:

"Well, stranger, if you are really of heavenly birth, like me, and if you are no robbers, I will give you the Fleece; but I must try you first. I bear no grudge against brave men. But the test of your courage and strength is a thing which I can do myself. I have two brazen-footed bulls that breathe fire from their mouths; these bulls I yoke, and drive over the ground, and when the furrows are made, I sow in them the teeth of a serpent, and a crop of armed men springs up: then I cut them down as they rise. If you can do this, you shall have the Golden Fleece, but not before: a brave man must not yield to a coward."

Jason was struck dumb with dismay. How could he do such a thing as this? But he put a bold face on it, and said after a little.

"I take your challenge, my lord King, even if I must die. Fate brought me here, and fates drives me on."

The King said: "Then make yourself ready for the task; and let me tell you, if you shrink, I will take care that another man shall tremble before he challenges his betters."

Jason went slowly out, along with his two comrades; and Argos followed him. Jason was a fine sight, young, handsome, and strong, with the bearing and air of a prince; Medeia looked at him stealthily, holding her veil aside, and her soul crept after him like a dream as he went, but Jason took no notice: he had not seen her yet.

Medeia, as I told you, was priestess of Hecatê, a grim goddess of darkness and night; she knew magic charms and spells, she was a witch in fact, but she did not think yet of this.   All she thought was:

"Poor boy! What a pity such a noble man should go to his doom. I hope he may escape! I pray to thee, my goddess, let him escape! But if not, he shall know that I am not glad, at least."

So she brooded over her trouble.

Meanwhile, Argos had remembered her too; and he said to Jason:

"I say, you have heard me tell of a girl who knows the secret spells of Hecatê, goddess of night. She is my mother's young sister, and I must try to get her to help."

"That is a good notion," said the young man, "do go and try; but it is a poor hope if we have to trust women to get us home."

Then he returned to his companions, and said:

"My friends, Aietas is simply furious; and he has set me a task to do—what do you think? He has two bulls that breathe fire; I must plow the soil with these, and sow dragons' teeth, which will grow up at once into armed men, and I must kill them all. I said yes—I could not help it, but what to do I don't know."

They were silent, and looked at one another in blank dismay. At last Peleus said:

"If you have the courage, make ready and do it.

If not, I will try myself. I can only die at the worst."

Others were ready too, for they were all brave men; but Argos said:

"We may come to that, but there is another thing to try first, so wait a little longer. There is a girl here who knows all the spells and charms of Hecatê, and she could make the bulls harmless, and master the devilish crop of the dragons' teeth. If you allow me, I will see what I can do with her."

Then Mopsos the prophet said: "Yes, do try; you remember that Phineus told us that we should return home by the help of the goddess of Love. It was her gentle bird, the dove, which led us through the Crashing Rocks, and this is a sign from heaven for us to trust. Let us appeal to Aphroditê!"

Indeed, Aphroditê was the girl's friend, although they knew it not. She had taught Medeia the charm of the wryneck, and brought it down from heaven to earth for the first time. This is a little speckled bird, which can move its head back without moving its body, like a snake. People used to spread it over a fourspoke wheel, wings and legs tied to the spokes, and twist the wheel round and round to bring their lover rolling back. You have a toy like that now, when the wheel is spun by a thread by pulling the two ends. Medeia first learned this charm, and others which you will hear of by-and-by.

So Jason pulled the Argo out of hiding, and moored her close to the shore, and Argos went back to the city.

Then Aietas held a meeting with his councillors, and told them that as soon as the bulls had made an end of Jason, they were to attack the pirates, and burn their ship, and punish their proud schemes. He told them to watch carefully; his father Helios had prophesied secret treachery from his family, and that is why he had sent the sons of Phrixos home over the sea. But he never thought of his daughters, Chalciopê and Medeia.

Argos prayed and pleaded with his mother Chalciopê, but she was afraid; and meanwhile Medeia had fallen asleep and seen a horrible dream. She woke up, and cried:

"O how unhappy I am! I tremble for the stranger—but let him take a wife out of his own people, and leave me here to be a maiden for ever. Yet I will see if my sister can comfort me!"

She went to the door of her room, then came back ashamed, then went again and again, and threw herself on her bed face downwards, and wept. One of her maids noticed her, and ran to tell her sister Chalciopê, who was then sitting with her son, and wondering what to do. But this tale brought her at once to Medeia's bedside, and she said:

"Why do you cry like that, Medeia my own? How I wish we were both far away from this dreadful place!"

Medeia flushed, and for a long time she could not speak a word; but at last she told half her secret—

"O my sister! I have had a horrible dream, and

I am afraid that our father will kill your boys along with the strangers! God forbid—I hope you may never have to mourn for your sons!"

That gave Chalciopê a chance, and she said at once:

"I am afraid too, and that is why I have come to you now. Can't you do something to help? But promise me you will keep secret what I say, or I shall come back a ghost from the house of death, and haunt you with my boys!"

"What can I do?" said Medeia. She said:

"Can't you help the stranger to do his task, for the sake of my sons? Argos has come to implore my help, I left him in my room."

Then Medeia's heart bounded with joy, and her cheeks flushed, and a mist swam before her eyes, as she cried:

"My dear, I will do it! May I die myself, if I think of anything rather than you and your boys, my dear kinsmen and companions. I am your sister, and I am your daughter too, for you often lifted me to your breast as a baby, as my own mother told me. But be silent! and before dawn, I will bring a charm against the bulls."

Then Chalciopê left Medeia, terrified and ashamed that she should help another man against her own father. Darkness came over the world, but Medeia could not sleep; her heart throbbed and quivered within her breast, as the sun flashes quivers of light on water when you pour it into a pail. Now she thought she would give the charm, now she would not, but die in silence.

"O that I had never seen him!" she thought. "Let him die, if that is his fate! How can I help—how can I go against my father? No! let me be stoned, let me die, but only let him go safe!"

At last she made up her mind. She brought out her casket, full of drugs:

"Ah!" she said, "that one will give me peaceful death!" And she put out a hand to take it—but fear of the dark house of Hadês held her back, and what might come in that dark hall. Then she put by her casket, and waited watching for the dawn.

When dawn came, she gathered up her golden hair, and bathed her cheeks, and smoothed her skin with ointment; then donning a beautiful robe, she threw a silvery veil about head and shoulders, and called her maids. These were twelve girls of her own age; and she bade them put the mules to the wagon, to carry her to Hecatê's temple. She took from her casket a charm which they call the charm of Prometheus. If any one should sacrifice by night to Hecatê and use this charm, all the coming day he could not be cut with metal or scorched with fire, but for that day he would be unconquerable. It was named because it grew first when the ravening eagle dropt on the earth some of the ichor of Prometheus; ichor in the gods is what blood is in man, and these drops came from the liver when that eagle tore it out. The plant grows on two stalks, a cubit high, with a yellow flower like a crocus: the root in the earth looks like flesh newly cut. She had gathered the dark juice

the daughter of Minos, in kindness rescued Theseus
from the monstrous man-bull Minotaur; she left her
native land and went aboard ship with him—and
Ariadnê's crown has been placed among the stars!
So the gods will thank you, if you save us.   One so
beautiful must surely have gracious gentleness in
you."

She dropt her eyes, with a smile, then looked
him straight in the face, and gave him the charm;
she would have given him her own soul.   They gazed
awhile at each other, and she said at last:

"Take care now to do what I tell you.   When my
father has given you the dragon's teeth, you must
wait until midnight, then bathe in the river, and
alone, clad in dark dress, dig a round pit; in the pit
kill a ewe, and sacrifice it whole, with the pyre heaped
over the pit.   Pour honey from a goblet, and pray
to Hecatê.   Then leave the pyre and go, but do not
turn or look back, if you hear footsteps or the baying
of hounds.   At dawn, mix this charm with water,
and rub your whole body with it as with oil: then
you will be a match for men and gods.   Sprinkle
also your shield and sword with it; then the spear
of the earth-born men shall not pierce you, and the
fire shall not burn you.   But this will last only one
day.

"Another thing I will tell you.   When the earth-
born men are springing up in the furrow, throw a
big stone among them; and they will fight over it,
and kill one another.   After that, you can get the
Fleece, and go wherever you will."

Then the tears ran over her cheeks, and she took his right hand, and said:

"Remember Medeia's name, when you return home, and I will remember yours far away. Tell me where your home is."

He said: "Indeed, I will never forget you, if I do escape, and if the King does not find us another task worse than this. My home is Iolcos, a city in a plain surrounded by mountains, a plain of good pasture, full of sheep, where Prometheus and his son first founded cities and built temples to the gods."

She said: "Only remember me, when you are at home in Iolcos, and I will remember you, whatever my father may wish. If you forget me, may a messenger-bird come and tell me—or may the storm-winds blow me over the sea, to sit in your hall an unexpected guest!"

She said this weeping, but Jason replied: "Let the storm-winds blow, my dear, no messenger-bird for me—that is only nonsense: but come to Hellas yourself, and you shall be welcomed and honoured by all, for you will bring husbands and sons back safe! And a wife you shall be in my hall, and nothing shall part us but death."

The maids were becoming anxious by this time, for evening drew near; but she lingered listening to his precious words, and gazing at him, until at last Jason said:

"It is time to go, or some one will notice, but we will meet here again."

So they parted; he returned to his comrades, and she passed through her maids without seeing them, for her soul was in the clouds. She drove back, and Chalciopê asked her questions: she did not hear, and she hardly spoke, but sat on a stool by her sister's couch, leaning her cheek on her hand.

Jason told his companions what had happened, and showed the charm; all were glad except Idas, who was angry still, for he wanted to fight the King. Next day, they sent two men to fetch the seed, Aithalidês the herald and Telamon. Aietas gave them the teeth of that dragon, which Cadmos found at Thebes, and killed there; he sowed some first on the Theban plain, and armed men sprang up and fought, but some were left alive and founded the Theban nation. The other teeth Aietas had, and he gave plenty now to be taken back to the ship, for he thought they would settle the business even if the cattle were yoked.

Jason had been making all ready; he got a ewe, and milk and honey, and found a place in a clear meadow. He bathed in the river, and put on a dark robe; he dug a pit of a cubit's depth, and piled it with billets of wood, and killed the ewe, and laid its body upon the pile; he kindled the wood, and poured in libations, praying to the dread goddess Hecatê: she heard him and came to the place, with twining serpents and burning torches and howling hounds of hell. The meadows trembled at her step, the spirits of marsh and river shrieked, and Jason was afraid—but he turned not nor looked until he came back to the place where his friends were. And now dawn arose.

Then King Aietas made ready. He donned a corselet which Arês had given him, and a golden helmet with four plumes, and he took a shield of many hides, and a spear terrible and unconquerable. His chariot was ready; he mounted and took the reins; then he drove to the place, with crowds following.

Meanwhile Jason sprinkled his own sword and spear and shield with the charm. His friends proved his weapons; no one could bend that spear, and when Idas angry still hewed with an axe at the butt, the edge was repelled as a hammer from the anvil. Then he rubbed his body, and felt a thrill of strength run through him: he leapt high in the air, tossing spear and shield. Then they rowed up the Argo to the place of trial, beyond the city; there they found King Aietas and the Colchians.

Jason leapt from the ship, and came forward with spear and shield, his sword slung round his shoulder, his body unprotected; he carried the helmet full of the dragon's teeth.

Aietas carried the plow of adamant; and now he plumped it down on the ground, and brought up the two brazen-foot bulls blowing fire from their mouths. Jason fixt the butt of his spear in the earth, and leaned his helmet against it, and walked towards the bulls. Both rushed at him together, breathing fire; but he set his feet well apart, and awaited their onset, holding the shield before him. They attacked him with their horns, but he stood fast, and the flames played about him but did him no harm. He grasped the horn of the right-hand bull and dragged it to the yoke, kicking behind the foreknees so that it fell, and so he threw also the other bull. Then he threw down the shield and held them, while his friends passed him the yoke. He bound their necks to it, and lifted the pole and tied the tip on to the yoke. Then he slung his shield behind his back, and caught up helmet and spear, and pricked the bulls under their flanks: he guided the plow on a straight furrow by its handle of adamant. The bulls drove on breathing blasts of fire and smoke, and he pressed the plow firmly with his foot, and sowed the dragon's teeth behind as he went.

When the third part of the day was left from dawn, he had finished his plowing; he loosed the bulls, and scared them back to the plain, while he went down to the river, and scooped up a drink of water in his helmet. By this time, the earth-born men were springing up all over the field, spears and shields and helmets were everywhere. Then Jason remembered Medeia's advice; and he picked up a big stone, and threw it among them, himself crouching down behind his shield. The Colchians roared in amazement, and Aietas could not make out what this meant. But he saw in a minute; for the earth-born ones leapt yelling upon each other and killed and killed—they fell by their own spears on their mother earth. Then Jason rushed upon them, and drew his sword, and mowed them down like hay—some half risen into the air, some showing a head as far as the shoulders, some just standing upright, some themselves rushing to battle. The furrows were filled with blood, as runnels of a spring with water. Aietas went back to the city sorrowful, and wondered what now he could do against the heroes.

IV

THE GOLDEN FLEECE

Aietas all night long was deliberating with his
council what he had better do to get rid of these
foreigners; and he was convinced in his mind that
his daughters had something to do with it, and
there was a plot against him. Medeia was in mortal
terror, for she was convinced that he knew something; she was afraid that her maids might let out
the secret. She would like to have taken poison
herself, but she put back all her drugs into the casket,
and kissed her bed, and stole out of the house, and
out of the city: locks and bars were nothing before
her magic power. She came to the riverside, and
saw on the opposite bank the fire of the Argonauts:
she called loudly to Phrontis, the youngest son of
Phrixos, and he and his brothers knew her voice,
and they rowed across for her. Jason and the boys
leapt ashore, and she cried:

"Save me, my friends—and yourselves too, for
all is brought to light. I will lull the dragon to
sleep. You shall have the Golden Fleece, only do
not desert me now!"

Jason gently raised her, and said: "Zeus and Hera

be witnesses that I will make you my own wedded wife, when we reach the land of Hellas."

She told them to row to the sacred grove, and they lost no time. By the altar which Phrixos had set up Jason and Medeia went ashore. They followed the path to a great oak tree, and there hung the Golden Fleece, shining red like a cloud under the rising sun. But before it lay a sleepless dragon, a huge dragon, in length and breadth not less than a ship of fifty oars: the sleepless eyes saw them, and he hissed so loud that he was heard miles away, and young mothers awoke, and clasped their newborn babes who stirred restless at the noise. He rolled his coils round and round; but Medeia came before him and called Sleep to her aid, and prayed to the queen of the night to help her. The dragon was charmed by her sweet voice, and stretched out his long body, and raised his grisly head: she sang and sang, and sprinkled him with a spray of juniper. He let his jaws sink down and lay motionless on the ground.

She went on smearing the monster's head with her charm, while Jason seized the Fleece: he threw it over one shoulder, and carried it carefully along to the ship. He laid it upon the deck, and covered it up, and seated Medeia in the stern as he spoke to them:

"Now, my friends, our task is done; let us return to our native land. This is our preserver, and she is to be my wife. Aietas will try now to bar our way, so you must row off at once—half of you row,

" Save me, my friends—and yourselves too."

the other half be ready to hold your shields over them."

Then he put on his armour, and cut the stern-hawsers, and they set off. In three days they were at the mouth of the river Halys, where Lycos their friend received them.

Aietas soon had his people on the chase in a fleet of ships, under Apsyrtos, his son, the brother of Medeia.

V

THE RETURN VOYAGE

Now they remembered that Phineus had told them they must return by another way, but they did not understand him clearly. Argos then spoke to them:

"There is another way home, which Phineus must have meant. We go to the river, Istros,[1] which rises in the Rhipaian Mountains, and runs towards us in this Inhospitable Sea, and also by another stream into the Trinacrian Sea,[2] which lies along your land, and there it is called Acheloios."

At these words, a trail of light appeared in the sky, a lucky portent; to show the way and the heroes cheered it loudly. So they left their friend Lycos, and sailed westwards with canvas outspread until they reached the mouth of Istros.

But the Colchian fleet divided. One part went past the Clashing Rocks and through the strait; the other entered a second mouth of the Istros, and crossed before Jason into the Ionian Sea, where the river discharging encloses an island, three-cornered,

[1] Danube.

[2] Sicilian, that is the Ionian Sea or Adriatic.

with its base opposite the coast and its point in the Sea. The Colchians came down through the southern mouth, and the heroes through the northern. When the country shepherds caught sight of these great ships, they ran away and left their sheep, for they had never seen such things before, and thought they were monsters of the deep.

So Apsyrtos blocked all the ways, and waited for Jason; and there would have been a battle, where Jason's crew, few against many, must have been destroyed, but they met and made an agreement. The Heroes might keep the Golden Fleece, because Aietas had so promised; but Medeia was to be given in ward to the goddess on the island of Artemis, until some wise King should hear the case and give judgement.

Medeia did not like this. She called Jason aside, and said:

"Have you forgotten your promises Jason? and your oaths by the suppliant's god? I have left my home, my country, my father, to save you! How did you master the fire-breathing bulls? How did you get the Golden Fleece? Because I believed you: and you are now in place of husband, and brother, and father to me. Take me away with you now, or now cut my throat with your sword! My curse will be upon you, the avenging Furies will follow you, you shall not sit long at ease with your friends for all your agreements!"

Jason said: "What can I do, my dear? I don't like it any more than you do. The Colchians are too many for us, and the people hereabouts are all on their side. But this agreement will be a net to catch them with, as you will see."

Then she said: "When wicked things are done, we must meet them with wicked plans. I will tempt Apsyrtos to come into your hands; you meet him with splendid gifts. Then kill him! and you can fight the Colchians without their leader."

So she invited her brother, and made up a tale, that the sons of Phrixos had given her to Jason against her will; and if he liked, he could take her now, and the Golden Fleece, and carry both back to Thesis. He came, and Jason prepared splendid gifts, one of them the crimson mantle which Hypsipylê had given him in Lemnos; it was a lovely fragrant robe, which had once belonged to the god Dionysos himself. So Apsyrtos came alone, by night, in one ship, to the island of Artemis, where he hoped she would tell him her plan. And Jason laid an ambush for him.

They met—Jason leapt out from hiding, and struck him down; he died, but in dying he smeared his blood on his sister's dress, and the Fury beheld the deed.

Medeia held up a torch: the waiting heroes closed in upon the one ship, and killed all the Colchians in it. Then they rowed away, taking Medeia with them, across to the mouth of Eridanos river.[1]

The Colchians now had no leader, and they did not know what to do; but they were afraid to go home, so in the end they dispersed and settled among

[1] Padus, or Po.

the neighbouring islands or on the mainland, where their descendants now are, calling themselves Apsyrtians or some other name. The Argonauts wandered about among neighbouring islands.

But Zeus was angry at the murder, and ordained that they must be cleansed by Circê, the sister of Aietas. But they did not know this. They sailed therefore past Corcyra, and past Melite,[1] and the island of Calypso; but storms drove them upon a rocky island, and as they went, the speaking beam in their stem, which Athena had put there, uttered a voice, and told them that Zeus was angry, and why; they should never reach home, until Circê should purify them. They were driven thence to the mouth of Eridanos, where the body of Phaëthon was burning still, and his sisters were weeping and wailing. They sailed up the river to the place where it meets the Rhodanos[2] and another river which runs north through Celtic lands[3]. They first took this northern river, but Hera turned them back, and they ran down the other river to the sea, and along the west coast of Italy, and at last they came to the harbour of Aiaia,[4] where they found Circê bathing her head in the sea.

[1] Now Meleda.

[2] Rhone.

[3] Rhine.

[4] The Circeian promontory on the Tyrrhenian Sea.

VI

CIRCÊ

CIRCÊ was a terrible witch, and the sister of King Aietas. She had been visited by a dreadful dream; the walls of her house seemed to be running with blood, and fire was burning up her magical herbs; she quenched the fire with blood, and woke up with a dizzy head, and went down to the sea to cool her head in the salt water. All about her were gambolling strange creatures, like a flock of sheep about the shepherd; but the creatures were not like sheep, but all mixt up, bodies and limbs, goats' heads and snakes' bodies, or little elephants with deer's legs; like the experiments of the old earth, which grew up out of the mud before the arms and legs were sorted out into decent animals. She used to drug men also with her magic herbs, and change them into lions and leopards or pigs—they were quite tame, and romped up purring or growling pleasantly, and wagging their tails, and doing no harm.

The heroes were astonished at the sight, and she went back to her house, waving her hand to beckon them. Jason and Medeia sat down on the hearth, as suppliants do: Jason drove into the ground the sword which had killed Apsyrtos, and Medeia covered her face with her hands, and they did not meet Circê's look. Then Circê understood what they wanted, and she began to offer the sacrifice to Zeus the god of suppliants, to cleanse them before they could approach his altar. To atone for the murder, she raised above their heads a sow taken from its litter, and killed it, and sprinkled their hands with the blood, and poured drink-offerings to Zeus, the Cleanser; then standing by the hearth, she burnt cakes of atonement without wine, and prayed that the Furies might stay their vengeance, and be gentle to repentant sinners.

Then Circê raised them up, and led them to seats, and asked them to tell her the story of their wanderings. Medeia now looked her in the face, and she knew her kinswoman, because all the children of the Sun shoot out from their eyes a golden gleam. Medeia told her all, but she did not speak of the murder of her brother. Then Circê said:

"This is an evil tale. Aietas will soon come even to Hellas to avenge this wrong; but you are my suppliant and my kinswoman, and I will do you no harm. Only take this stranger, whoever he is, and go; do not kneel to me, for I can never approve your doings."

Then Jason led her away, and they went back to the Argo. Iris told Hera they were going; and she gave her commands. So first she summoned Thetis to wait on Hera, and she told Hephaistos to still his blasts of fire until the Argo should pass by, and Aiolos was bidden to hold all the winds except the

All about her were gambolling strange creatures.

west wind, which was to waft them to the Phaiacian land.   Thetis came before Hera, and Hera said:

"My dear Thetis, you know how I cared for you as an infant, and how I found you a husband in the noblest of mortal men, Peleus; Zeus wanted you, and you refused, and I am always grateful.   Now you have a boy, Achilles, who is being cherished by that fine old fellow Cheiron the Centaur, and he will be most glorious of men; but when after death he comes to the Elysian plain, where all the good men are, it is fated that Medeia shall be his wife. I want you therefore to protect Medeia now, when Jason and she are to have a dangerous voyage.   Do you and your sisters see to it that they have a safe voyage, that Charybdis does not swallow them up, or Scylla catch their men.   Hephaistos will quench his fires, and Aiolos will make the west wind blow. Guide their ship when only a hairsbreadth is between them and destruction!"

Thetis answered: "If Hephaistos will quench his fires, and if Aiolos will stay his winds, we will see to it that he passes over the sea safely."

So she dived into the blue sea, and told her sisters of the deep to do their part; and she sped back to Aiaia, and found the heroes amusing themselves on the beach.   She drew near and touched the hand of Peleus her husband, but no one else could see her, then she said:

"Stay here no longer, my husband, but loose your hawser and set sail.   My sisters will guide your ship safely."

Peleus was amazed, for he had not seen her since she left him in anger over their baby boy, Achillês. She used to plunge him in fire in the night time, and by day she bathed him in ambrosia, the water of immortality, so that he might become immortal; but Peleus awoke, and saw his boy gasping in the flame—he uttered a loud cry, and she heard it, and threw her son screaming on the ground, and flew away like a breath of wind, and never again returned. So now he told his companions what Thetis had said, and next day they drew up the anchors and set sail.

They first passed by the island of the Sirens. These were partly like birds and partly like maidens, and they used to draw men to them by their sweet song. The heroes also were about to land, but Orpheus their minstrel twangled his harp, and sang a song so sweet that it drowned the Sirens; for his song could make the very trees caper and dance before him.

After this they came to the strait between Scylla and Charybdis: Scylla, with six long necks, and at the end of each a dog's head with deadly teeth; Charybdis, who sucked in the water till you could see the sand, and then spouted it out seething and steaming and showering spray. Past these they ran, and past the Wandering Rocks which blazed with fire. The waves tossed up the Argo like a ball into the air, and caught it again; and on the summit of the rock stood Hephaistos, leaning one shoulder on the handle of his hammer, and watched them. They ran past the island where Helios kept his cattle; they could see them as they passed, all white with golden horns. All day they sailed, and all night, and in the morning they came to the Phaiacian island.

Alcinoös the King gave them welcome; but the other host of Colchians now appeared, having made their way from Pontos by the strait. These would have carried off Medeia, but she cast herself on the Queen's mercy.

"Save me, O Queen! I have sinned, but I have repented, and I have been cleansed! And you, heroes, I saved you from those bulls, and gave you back to your homes, but I have lost my own home, wandering and accursed!"

The heroes promised not to forsake her; and the royal pair pondered all the night what they could do.

The Queen said: "This poor girl quite breaks my heart. She was deluded and distraught when she helped Jason to master the bulls; and she fears to fall into the hands of her father. Who is Aietas, after all? I know only his name, and he lives far away."

The King said: "It is not wise to despise Aietas; he may even make war upon us here. He is a great King. This is my judgement: If she is still a maid, I will send her back to her father; if she is a wife, she shall stay with her husband, and I think that is just."

In the morning, the herald took this message to Jason; and he at once arranged the wedding, and made Medeia his wife. They laid the Golden Fleece on the wedding couch; the nymphs of the rivers and trees brought fine linen, and wreaths of flowers; and the heroes were ready under arms in case there should be any attack.

Next day, Alcinoös went out to tell his judgement to the Colchians, and his men-at-arms went with him, and all the women watched, and the country people came out in crowds to see the sight. The Colchians then did not wish to make war with him, but they feared to go back to their King; so they also settled in another island. But the heroes had farther still to go.

They came in sight of the land of Pelops[1]; but the winds blew them across to Libya, into the dangerous gulf called Syrtis. They were driven right up on the shore, and they could see only sandbanks and sea behind, and desert and mist in front, a vast empty land, with no path, no river, no house. So they lay down as they were, on the sand, and the women wailed all night.

But the goddesses of Libya pitied them, and one drew Jason's cloak off his face, and told him not to despair:

"Up, man, and wake your fellows! When Amphitritê[2] shall have unyoked Poseidon's car, pay to your mother a recompense for her toil and labour with you, and you shall yet see home again."

[1] Peloponnesos.

[2] Wife of Poseidon.

Jason woke the others, all squalid with dust, and said: "I have seen three goddesses of this country, clad in goatskins from neck to knee; who said, Rise, and pay your mother a recompense for all her labour and travail with you, when Amphitritê shall have unyoked Poseidon's car. I do not rightly understand what they mean; but they say we shall see our home again. Then the mist hid them from my sight."

As he spoke, a great horse leaped from the waves upon the shore, with a golden mane flowing about his neck, and started swiftly to run his course. Then Jason said: "I think Poseidon's car has now been unyoked by his wife Amphitritê, and I think our mother is the Argo herself. She has carried us in her body, and suffers in our behalf. Then we will take her on our shoulders and carry her over the sand, where the horse's hooves will show us the way."

So they took the ship Argo over the sands; but how they did it, I do not know: whether by rollers which they set before the keel, or by long poles on their shoulders, for they were stronger men than we are. But however it may be, they carried Argo across the sands for twelve days and twelve nights, by crushing labour, to the shore of the Tritonian Lake. They passed the garden of Atlas, where grew the tree with golden apples, guarded by a monstrous dragon; but the dragon lay there dead, for Heraclês had killed it, and the nymphs Hesperidês lamented around the tree, but as the heroes

A great horse leaped from the waves upon the shore.

drew near, they became pillars of earth where they stood.

"Give us water, we pray you!" the heroes cried. And one of them said:

"That accursed man, who stole our apples and killed the dragon—he came but yesterday; a grim cruel man, with eyes flashing under a scowling brow, with a lionskin thrown over his shoulders; he carried a bow, and shot this great creature. He too was parched with thirst; he could find none, until he kicked at a rock beside the Tritonian lake, and water gushed out. He leaned both hands and chest on the ground, and drank stooping like a wild beast."

They gladly ran to the spot, and found the spring, and drank deep. All ran to search for Heraclês, but found no trace of him, for the wind had blown sand into his footsteps. Mopsos indeed perished: for prophesying cannot avert death. He trod on a serpent lying in the sand, and the serpent writhed round and bit him.

They launched the Argo into the Tritonian lake, and three days they sailed seeking for an outlet, but found none. Then a Triton appeared to them, and pointing with his hand, he said:

"That is your way yonder, a narrow channel of deep water amid all these banks of sand. Keep close to the shore, while it runs to the north; but when it bends, your way is clear over the sea to the land of Pelops, beyond Crete."

He lifted up a clod of earth, and said:

"Poseidon is my father, and I am Eurypylos who

rules the land of Libya. I welcome you as my guests, and I would do the proper thing if I could—I would give you a good dinner to begin with, and a good gift afterwards. I cannot feed you on sand, and you are in haste, I see: but here is my gift which I give to my guests, the earth of Libya. Take good care of it, and plant it in your home when you get there."

Euphemos stept down from the prow, and took the gift in his right hand; and Father Zeus made a loud thunderclap for an omen of good. They hung up the anchor at the prow, and set sail. Relays of guardians were set, to keep the clod safe; but they were all tired out with their hard work, and they did not keep it safe. When the coastline turned, the west wind fell, and they had to row; all night they rowed, and the next day they saw the coast of Crete.

But Crete was guarded by a huge man of bronze, whose name was Talos; and he would have destroyed them by hurling huge rocks, but Medeia stood on the prow and sang her magical songs, and Talos fell down and moved no more. They beached the Argo for that night, and went on in the morning.

Meanwhile amid all these labours, the clod of earth dropt overboard, and the waves took it to the island of Thera, where it remained for its fate in later days. That is another story, a long one, about Battos the Stutterer, who asked at Delphi how to amend his stammering tongue, and fate brought him from Thera to the land of Libya after thirteen generations: there he founded a great city called Cyrenê, which grew to wealth by the famous plant called silphium, which has been lost out of the earth.

After that, the Argo sailed on in safety, touching on the coast of Aegina, and at last she reached her home in Pagasai.

VII

THE CALYDONIAN BOAR

WHAT became of all these heroes, when they returned
with their Golden Fleece? They were a remarkable set
of men, who left their mark on the nation. I could
tell you stories about them all, but I will take first a
famous adventure, the hunt of the Calydonian Boar.

Oineus was King of Calydon in north Greece;
his wife was named Althaia, and among their children were two that I want to tell you about, a boy
Meleagros, who comes in this particular story, and
a girl Deianeira, who comes in another one.

The people were grateful to their gods, for giving
them good crops and fruits and sheep and cattle;
so they used to show their thanks by sacrificing the
firstfruits of everything every year. But one year
Oineus forgot Artemis: he made sacrifices to all the
other gods, but Artemis was left out, and she was
not one to forget an insult. She sent upon the
country a huge wild boar, such a monster as never
was seen in the world. His eyes were red with
blood and blazed like fire; his hard neck was covered
with sharp bristles, which stood up straight like rows
of spikes. Hot foam from his mouth covered his
chest and forelegs, and his teeth stuck out like the

tusks of an elephant. As he snorted, thunderbolts seemed to issue from his mouth. He trod down the growing crops, he spoilt the wheat in the ear; the farmers were in despair to see the ruin of their harvest. He rooted up the trees, and threw them down on the ground; there lay olives with their grey berries, apples and pears with their round green fruit. Then he ran riot among the flocks and heards, sheep and goats and cattle; neither bulls could defend them, nor herdsmen with dogs and stones. In fact, the country people all ran for it, and took refuge behind the walls of the cities.

Meleagros now gathered all the strongest young men he could find, and among them his old companions in the Quest of the Golden Fleece. Castor and Polydeuces came at once, Castor the horseman and Polydeuces the boxer. Jason was there himself, and Theseus with his bosom friend Peirithoös, Idas the sprinter and Lynceus the sharpsighted, Telamon and Peleus the father of Achillês, Nestor not yet an old man but young and strong, Amphiaraos the great seer, and many others: last of all, Atalanta, the only woman who had part in the great quest, a woman as good as any man, with her ivory quiver, and her hair knotted into a bob on her neck.

They tracked their boar to a valley, full of fine old trees, with a lake in the middle and several streams flowing into it, amid clumps of reeds and lush meadows and sedge. Nets were set up all round, the hounds were held all about in leash, as they followed the slot. The boar rushed out, crushing down the trees, and shouts arose, as the hunters discharged their arrows and held spears ready to receive him. He scattered the dogs, and threw down the men who stood up to him. One shot grazed a shoulder, others went wide. Jason hit him, but made no wound. This provoked the boar, and he belched out fire from his jaws and bowled over two men, killing a third; another jumped up on a tree and saved himself. The boar ran at the tree, and tried to cut it down with his tusks, while the young man sat above and watched him. Telamon gave chase, but stumbled over a root and fell; and while Peleus was helping him up, Atalanta let fly a shot and hit the boar under the ear. Meleagros saw the blood run, and called to the others: "Shame on you boys! Let a woman beat you!" They showered their spears upon the boar, but too carelessly, and they were caught in the branches. Then Ancaios cried aloud: "See what a man can do!" and lifted his axe; but the boar got in first and ran him through the body. Peirithoös raised his hunting spear, and ran at him, but Theseus cried out: "O my heart's friend, take care! Ancaios was too rash, and his courage was his death; stay behind, brave men can dare to shoot from a distance!" He tried a shot himself, but missed. Jason threw also, and hit an innocent dog by mistake. At last Meleagros cast two spears, and one struck full in the boar's back. The boar spun round and round in agony, and Meleagros ran his hunting spear right through the shoulder.

The monster lay stretched dead on the ground and

all thronged to see. Meleagros, with a foot resting upon the beast's head, spoke out:

"The prize is mine, for I killed him; but you, Atalanta, drew first blood, and you shall share it with me." Then he presented her with head and skin. She was pleased at that, as you may imagine, but the others were not; the two brothers of Althaia were angry above the rest, and one seized the spoils, saying boldly:

"Let be, girl, and do not steal our prize! If Meleagros will not keep it, then we are his natural heirs!"

A great quarrel arose, such a hullabaloo that we cannot see the rights of it, but in the end we find the Calydonians at war with their neighbours, the Curetians; the Calydonians were shut up in the city, and Meleagros sulked in his house and would not fight. He said it was much nicer to stay at home with his wife. The chief men of Calydon came and begged him to help; they offered him great domains and splendid gifts, but he would not. Old King Oineus came and begged him to help; he stood in the doorway and shook the leaves of the door, but the man would not. Mother and sisters begged him to help, but he would not. At last his wife Cleopatra threw her arms round his neck, and warned him of the horrors that would follow when the enemy broke in,—and they were breaking in, and fire was touching even his own walls—and he gave way. He went out and led his people to victory, but he killed his mother's brother.

Althaia was doing sacrifice in the temple for her son's victory, when she saw them carrying in her brother's dead body, killed by Meleagros her son! She was enraged, and cursed him. She knelt and beat her hands on the earth, calling upon Hades the King of the dark house of death, and his Queen awful Persephoneia, when suddenly she remembered something.

Long ago, when the boy was born, she saw the three Fates enter her room, the three dreadful sisters, Spinner and Lotter and Never-turn-back, tall women in black robes with gloomy faces; and Spinner said:

"Look at your brand burning upon the hearth; when it is burnt out, your son shall die."

Althaia leapt up in horror, and caught up the burning brand, and quenched it, and then laid it away carefully in her dower-chest; there it had been kept ever since. Now she ran home, and opened the chest, and there lay the half-burnt brand. She took it, and cast it on the fire; and as it burnt, Meleagros felt fire eating away inside him, and he fell down and died.

His mother in despair thrust a dagger into her own heart; and her sisters wept over their brother's ashes, until Artemis was satisfied at last and gave them a peaceful end; for she turned them into speckled guinea-fowl, and in this shape they twitter and cluck for ever.

VIII

ATALANTA AND THE GOLDEN APPLES

AND what became of Atalanta?

Her father had wanted a son, and when Atalanta was born, he said: "What's the use of a girl to me? Put her out on the mountains, and let her die." So the servants put her out on the mountains. There a she-bear came along, and took a fancy to the strange little thing, and fed her with her own milk. By and by some hunters passed that way, and found her, and saved her, and brought her up.

She became a hard woman, like her hard father, and like the hard life she was forced to lead. She cared for no hardship, she shrank from no toil, she feared no wild beast of the forest. Even when two terrible Centaurs attacked her, she cared nothing, but killed them both. When she grew up, she found out her father, and came to live in his house. She made a great name for herself, in running and wrestling and other manly sports; she even wrestled with Peleus, and beat him. She must have been a handful to manage; so her father soon became tired of her, and did his best to find a husband who would relieve him of his troublesome daughter. At first she would not hear of a husband; but at last she agreed, on certain conditions.

The conditions were, that if anyone wanted to marry her, he must run a race with her; if he lost the race, he was to lose his life. But she was so beautiful, that many young men were willing to try, even on those terms; many did try, and failed, and they were put to death.

One young man, named Meilanion, a fine young fellow, laughed at this. "What fools you are," said he, "to run such a risk for a girl! Are there not plenty of girls in the country? You will not catch me risking my neck for one, no matter how beautiful she may be."

"That is all very well," said the young men, "but you have not seen her. Come with us to the next race, and then you may talk." "All right," he said, "I will come," and he went with them to see the race.

There they stood at the starting-post: Atalanta, like Artemis herself, as beautiful and as hard; and the young man, full of strength and grace, and confident that he would win. Off they went: he was quick on his feet, but nothing to Atalanta, who sped off like the wind, and easily came in first. Then the young man was led off to his death.

But would you believe it, no sooner had Meilanion set eyes on Atalanta, than he fell in love as deeply as the rest. He thought he had never seen anything so beautiful as Atalanta, and on the spot he declared that he would try his luck. Atalanta herself was sorry, as she saw this fine young man. "You are only a boy," she said, "and why should you throw your life away? Think how many lives have been wasted already!" For she had grown tired of this; indeed, she thought the condition would have kept men away, and all she wanted was to be left alone. But in fact, she fell a little in love with Meilanion too, and she did her best to dissuade him. Why she did not accept him at once, if she liked him, I do not know; but perhaps she felt that it would make her look small before the world, and she did not really love him enough, as yet. So a day was fixed for the new race.

Meilanion was not quite so cheerful when he got away. He did not feel so sure he would win; and now that he could not see her, he did not feel so sure she was worth it. But he felt he could not back out of the challenge. Then he prayed to the goddess Aphroditê to help him, and she heard his prayer; for she did not like this hard maiden, who made light of the goddess of love. She had a wonderful tree in her grove, which bore golden apples; three of these apples she picked, and gave them to Meilanion, and told him what to do.

The day came. There were crowds of people to see the race: the king was there, with his court; Atalanta was there, girt in a short tunic, like Artemis, and ready to run. Meilanion came, with the golden apples tucked into a corner of his tunic. They made rather a bulge, but no one noticed it in all that excitement.

She caught sight of the bright thing, and hesitated.

The two runners stood at the starting-point: the signal was given—they were off. Atalanta did not run as swiftly as usual, for her own heart weakened a little, to see this beautiful young man running for his life. For a little time, they ran neck and neck; but the ardour of the race took hold of Atalanta, and she shot ahead.

Then Meilanion pulled out one of his apples, and rolled it ahead of Atalanta. She caught sight of the bright thing, and hesitated, and stopped in her course to pick it up. Meilanion passed her, and sped away at full speed. But Atalanta tucked her apple into her bosom, and off she went again; she soon passed Meilanion, and left him behind her. Now Meilanion pulled out another apple, and sent it rolling a little to one side. Once more Atalanta saw the apple, and darted away from the course to pick it up; once more Meilanion ran ahead, and this time he gained a good deal of ground.

But the pace was telling on Meilanion. He began to pant, and his breath came dry from his throat; run as he would, he could not keep ahead, and now he took out his last apple. This time, he threw it as hard as he could, right away to one side, but so that Atalanta could see it. And as before, Atalanta darted in pursuit, and ran right out of the course until she was able to catch it, and tuck it away with the rest.

They were not yet at the end of the race, and Atalanta began to gain on Meilanion; but Aphroditê was watching, unseen, and she made the apples grow heavier and heavier, until Atalanta felt as if she were carrying a weight of lead in her bosom. She went slower and slower, and Meilanion kept ahead, and won the race.

Then there were great rejoicings, and Atalanta was no less pleased than the rest, although she did not say much about it. So they were married, and they deserved to live happily ever after, but unluckily they did not. For they gave offence to Zeus, and he turned them into a pair of lions. Perhaps after all, Atalanta was more happy as a lioness than she would have been as a woman, but we do not know her side of the story, because she could no longer tell it.

IX

PELEUS

ANOTHER hero had already an adventurous history.

He was the son of Aiacos, prince of Aegina, who was himself a son of Zeus. Aegina is a very important island in Greek history, and the heroes who were of the family of Aiacos played a great part. Aiacos himself was a just man; so that he was even asked to settle disputes among his kinsmen, the Immortals, and after death, he became one of the Judges of the dead, in the dark house of Hades.

Once upon a time, when Peleus was hunting on Mount Pelion, a certain prince hid the sword of Peleus as he slept, and left him alone among the wild beasts. There he would have perished, for the Centaurs caught him; but old Cheiron the Centaur saved his life, and afterwards found his sword. For some time after that, he lived with Cheiron, and hunted the wild beasts.

There was a sea-nymph, named Thetis, who was so beautiful that two of the great gods fell in love with her. One was Poseidon, lord of the sea, who knew all the Nereids that lived in the coral caves under the waters; but he had never seen the equal of Thetis, and he wanted to make her his wife. The other god was Zeus himself.   No doubt he had heard Poseidon talking about this young beauty, and went to have a look at her himself.

At all events, the brothers fell out about it; and as they could not agree, they asked the advice of the wise Themis, the goddess of justice and law. She said at once: "Before I give my opinion, I ought to tell you one thing: her son will be stronger than his father.   I should advise you to let her marry a mortal man, and that will be better for both of you."

The gods were persuaded at once.   "No stronger sons for me," said Zeus, "that is my view, whatever you may think of it, brother Poseidon."   "I agree with that," said Poseidon.   "Well, who shall be her husband?"   Zeus answered: "She shall have a good one, and I know a man who has lately distinguished himself by honourable conduct, one Peleus, who is living at present with old Cheiron in his cave."

Then a message was sent to Peleus, telling him that Zeus was ready to give him a beautiful nymph of the sea, on condition that he must catch her first. Cheiron told him about it.   He said: "Like the other creatures of the sea, she can change her shape.   If you want her for a wife, you must catch her, and hold her fast."

Peleus felt sure he would win.   Perhaps he had learnt something from his wrestling match with Atalanta; but at least he knew now that the gods were on his side.   So he went down to the seashore with Cheiron; and there was Thetis, waiting for him; there were the nymphs of the sea, all looking on; and there were the gods, as pleased as possible to see a new kind of wrestling match.

Peleus caught hold of the two wrists of Thetis, and held fast. Thetis changed first into a tree, and he held fast to the two branches he found in his hands; that was easy enough. Next, she became an eagle, and he held her two wings. And then suddenly he found himself holding the strong paws of a tiger. Still he would not let go; and now he was holding a great lion. I suppose Thetis was losing her patience, for the next thing she did, was to change into wind. I do not know how he held the wind, but he did, and so he did when she changed into fire, which scorched him, and then water, which put out the fire. His hands were still clenched, when he saw that he held two of the long arms of a giant squid. But that was a mistake on the part of Thetis; for he held these arms so tight, that she could not change any more, and so she became at last Thetis.

Now Thetis knew that she was beaten, so she put a good face on the matter, and agreed to be married to Peleus. And it was indeed a magnificent wedding, which was remembered all through Greek history. There was a grand feast, there were visitors from far and near, and to cap all, there was a half-circle of noble thrones, and the gods themselves seated upon them, to share in the feast, while the Muses sang and played on the flute and harp, and the Seasons danced in the midst. The Fates also sang,

the Spinner, the Portioner, and Never-turn-back.
They sang:

"Fortunate pair! Your child shall be a boy
Who shall lay low the enemy hosts at Troy.
No other man shall be so brave and strong.
Run on, my spindles, pull the thread along!"

Cheiron gave Peleus a great ashen spear, which we often hear of in the stories about him; Poseidon gave him two immortal horses, named Chestnut and Bay, and the other gods gave him weapons and armour.

Peleus had now got his wish, and a divine wife; but he found out, as many men have done, that it is better to marry one of your own rank in life. Thetis bore a son, Achillês, and she loved him very much, but she wanted to make him immortal, like herself. She dipped him in the awful river of Styx, to make his body safe against wounds; but she had to hold him by the heel and ankle, and so his heel was left unprotected, and it was a wound in the heel that killed him in the end. Not content with a water-bath, she used fire too. Every night she used to lay him in the fire, as Demeter did to another baby, if you remember; this was done to burn away all of him that was mortal, and in the day she used to anoint him with the gods' own ambrosia, which made them immortal. But one night Peleus caught her at it, and when he saw the child writhing amid the flames, he cried out. Then Thetis caught up the child, and threw him down on the ground, and fled away shrieking to the sea: into the sea she plunged, and returned to her father Nereus and the sea-nymphs her sisters, and came back no more. Peleus lived sad and deserted in his palace halls.

But he took the child Achillês, and gave him over to Cheiron to train him up. Cheiron fed him on the marrow of lions, to make him brave and strong, and on the marrow of stags, to make him swift of foot; he became so swift, that he could catch any animal by running after it, and he was always called by everyone Swiftfoot Achillês. When he grew older, Cheiron made him a little sword and a little spear and a little shield, and little bow and arrows, and sent him out to catch what he could. So he practised the arts of war on mice and moles, which he was to practise later in real battle.

But the poor old man was left lonely in his great hall; for he had only one son, the little Achillês, whom we saw in his nurse's arms on the day when the Argo was launched. Achillês grew up to be the great Grecian hero in the war before Troy, which Homer sings of, and in his last days he described his father's fate.

"Zeus has two jars," he says, "of the gifts that he gives, standing upon the floor beside him, one of good things, and one of evil things. When the Thunderer mixes and gives, a man meets with good sometimes and bad other times: when he gives all bad, he makes the man despised and rejected; grinding misery drives him over the face of the earth, and he walks without honour from gods or from men. And so with Peleus, the gods gave him glorious gifts from his birth, for he was pre-eminent in the world for wealth and riches, he was King over the Myrmidons and although he was mortal they made a goddess his wife. But God gave him evil too, because he got no family of royal princes in his palace, but only one son, to die before his time. And now he is growing old, and I cannot care for him; for I am here in Troy, troubling you, Priam, and your children."

And what the little boy did, and how he quarrelled with Agamemnon his king, and how his fiery soul was tamed at last, you will read in the moving story of Homer.

X

HERACLES

We left Heraclês hurrying off to help his page Hylas, who was seized by a water-nymph and dragged down into her fountain. The Argo sailed away without him, and they were told by a god of the sea not to turn back, because Heraclês was fated to carry out his great work—his Labours, and the destruction of monsters all over the world. He was the greatest of all heroes, all the sons of gods and mortal women.

He was the son of Zeus and Alcmene, princess of Thebes, and there was great excitement over his birth. Hera was jealous and angry; and as soon as he was born, with his twin-brother Iphiclês, she sent two large serpents into the chamber, to kill the babies. But Heraclês lifted up his head, and clutched the throats of the two serpents, and held them writhing until their lives were throttled out of them. Up jumped his mother, and ran to help, and all the women shrieked out: "He's dead!" In came the men, clad in full armour, in came prince Amphitryon, holding a drawn sword in his hand. When he saw the baby Heraclês, with a serpent hanging limp from each hand, he cried out: "Who told me the baby was dead? It is the serpents that are dead!" But glad as he was, there was something about it which he could not understand; so he went to find old Teiresias, the Theban seer, who lived next door. "Come out, neighbour!" he said, "what does this mean?" And Teiresias told him by prophecy the mighty deeds which the baby was destined to do when he grew up. "And now," he went on, "gather up twigs of briar and wild pear, and with these burn the bodies of these two serpents; and let some one take up the ashes, and throw them into the river, and return without looking behind him; then the river shall carry them out of your country into the sea."

So Heraclês grew up; and the best masters taught him to shoot arrows from the bow, and to box, and wrestle, and fight in every manner, and to read and write, to sing and to play upon the harp. Prince Amphitryon taught him to drive the chariot, and Castor himself, the horseman god, taught him how to manage a horse, and to use the sword and the javelin, and to fight in armour, and how to lead men in time of war.

So he grew up till his eighteenth year, and then a surprising thing happened. He was thinking what his future life was likely to be; probably he had heard something of the prophecies of Teiresias, and perhaps he shrank from the danger a little. But he saw, or he thought he saw, two women approaching him. And one of them ran in front, to get the first word; and he saw that she was tall and handsome, and decked out in gay finery, with her cheeks rather too red to be natural; and she said to him: "Young man, I see you are in doubt what to do, and what path of life to follow. I invite you to follow me; you shall have the easiest and pleasantest life in the world, no hard work and no dangers; you shall eat, drink, and be merry, others shall work and you shall have the enjoyment, and you shall be as happy as the day is long." And Heraclês said: "What is your name?" The woman answered: "My real name is Pleasure, but my enemies call me Vice."

By this time, the second woman had come up. Heraclês saw this one also to be tall and handsome, but after a different fashion; for she was stately and dignified, and of a noble look; her dress was all white, truth was in her eyes, and modesty in her manners. She said: "Young sir, I know your parents and your breeding, and how you have been educated and brought up; which makes me hope that you will be a good workman of noble deeds. I will not deceive you with promises of pleasant things, but I will tell you the truth. Nothing that is really good can be got without labour and hardship, for so the gods have ordained. If you wish to enjoy the fruits of the earth, you must plough and sow, and reap and mow. So if you wish your body to be strong, you must make your body the servant to your mind, and fear not labour and sweat. And just in the same way, if you wish for the gods' favour, you must serve the gods; if you wish for the love of friends, you must do good to your friends; if you wish for honour from your city or your native land, you must work for their benefit, and you must defend them from enemies without and tyrants within. Follow me, and I can make you great, and truly happy." Heraclês said: "And what is your name?" She answered: "My name is Virtue."

Then Pleasure said: "See, Heraclês, what a hard road she puts before you! Not a scrap of pleasure in it!" But Virtue said: "Such pleasure as hers leads only to surfeit and weariness; he that tries to be happy, never succeeds; but he that does noble deeds gains happiness without trying."

And Heraclês resolved to follow the hard road, and to put away from his mind the craving for pleasure.

So Heraclês made his choice. But his first task was to master himself, before he could do great deeds with his own strength; for he had a violent temper. And so once he quarrelled with his music-master, who found fault with him, and struck him; then Heraclês lifted up his harp, and struck the man down, and killed him. He was not found guilty of murder, since the other had struck first, but Prince Amphitryon sent him to work on the cattle-farm, that he might school himself and master his temper. While he was there a lion came down from the hills and attacked the cattle; but Heraclês killed the lion, called the Lion of Cithairon, which was the name of the hill country whence he came.

After this he gathered together the young men of

the city of Thebes, and they fought against a neighbouring King who held Thebes under tribute, and set Thebes free from the tribute; for which the King of Thebes, whose name was Creon, gave Heraclês his daughter Megara for a wife.

But soon after this a terrible misfortune happened to Heraclês; for madness came upon him, sent by the goddess Hera, who was always his enemy: and Heraclês in his madness killed his own children. When he recovered, he sought how he might atone for his deed, and asked the oracle at Delphi what he should do. The oracle told him that he must live at Tiryns, an ancient city in South Greece, and for years he must serve Eurystheus King of Mycenai and do what he commanded. Each year therefore Eurystheus set him a hard task to do, and these are called the Twelve Labours of Heraclês.

(1) The First Labour was the Nemean Lion. There was a terrible lion that ranged on the mountains not far from Tiryns. You should look up this country on the map, for it comes often into the stories of Greece. There is a fertile plain on the east side of Greece, looking towards Asia, which contained three ancient cities, built in the beginning of time by great warriors who came from Asia. Near the coast is the first, Tiryns, and you may see the ruins there to this day; for it was built of huge stones, and every one who sees it is amazed. In the middle of the plain is a large rock, and upon this the second city was built, named Argos; and at the end of the plain is the third city, Mycenai, which is also to be

seen still, in ruins, with a wonderful gate, built of huge stones, called the Lion Gate, because above it are the figures of two lions rampant. The whole plain is called the plain of Argos.

Now at Mycenai the hills and mountains begin; and a few miles from it is the valley of Nemea, where this lion of Nemea used to range about. This lion was of huge size; he was a son of the monster Typhon, and he could not be wounded with iron, or bronze, or stone. He had a den in one of the rocks, a long tunnel with two openings, where he used to live; and if he were chased he ran into one end, and ran out of the other. Eurystheus commanded Heraclês to bring him the skin of this lion.

So Heraclês took with him his bow, and a quiver full of arrows, and a heavy club which he used to carry. When he came to the place, he could find no tracks, nor could he ask news from anyone, for all the people were afraid to come out and there was no one in the fields. Towards evening, the lion came to his den full fed, with his mouth and chest all spotted with blood, and licking his chaps. Heraclês hid by the way, and let fly a shaft at him; but the arrow slid off his skin, for he could not be wounded by iron, or bronze, or stone. Heraclês shot him again, full in the chest, but the arrow fell useless to the ground. The lion rolled his eyes, and saw Heraclês; then lashing his flanks with his tail, he gathered himself up for a spring. As he leapt, Heraclês held up his left arm wrapt in his cloak, and brought down his

club with a bang on the lion's head; the club splin-
tered in fragments, but it checked the spring, and
the lion stood wagging his head and dizzy with the
blow. Then Heraclês threw down his bow and
arrows, and leapt on the lion's back, treading down
the lion's hind-legs with his own feet, while he put
his hands round the lion's neck, and pulled up one
foreleg; then he got this leg under his arm, and gripped
the lion's throat with his two hands, and bending
him backwards, throttled him.

There lay the lion dead on the ground; but how
could Heraclês skin him? No iron could cut the
skin, no bronze, and no stone: but a thought came
into his mind, that he should cut off the skin of the
lion with the lion's own claws. And so he did.
He brought back the skin to Eurystheus, but he
would not give it up; and ever after that he wore
that skin as a garment, with the forepaws over his
shoulder, and the head like a helmet over his own
head, which looked out of the lion's jaws. This is
what you always see in the pictures of Heraclês.

(2) The Second Labour was the Lernaean Hydra.
There was a marsh in the plain of Argos called Lernai,
and in it there was a huge serpent with nine heads,
called Hydra the Watersnake, because she lived in
the marsh; and her middle head was immortal.
Some say she had a hundred heads, and it is difficult
to say how many there were, you will soon hear
why. Heraclês was commanded to kill this Hydra;
so off he went in a chariot, driven by his charioteer,
Ioläos, his nephew. When they came to the place,

Heraclês jumped out, and shot the serpent with his arrows, but she did not seem to mind that; then he attacked her with his club, but she did not mind that; then he took a sickle, and cut off head after head, but whenever he cut off one head, two grew in its place.

As he was cutting away, he felt a nip on his leg, and what should he see but an enormous crab come to help his friend the serpent. "That is not fair, two to one!" said Heraclês. "Ioläos, come and help me!" So Ioläos came with another sickle, but that only made matters worse. Suddenly Heraclês had a happy thought. "Get me some sticks," he said, "and burn the place!" Ioläos made a fire, and brought up the brands; and as Heraclês cut off a head, Ioläos burnt the place so that new ones could not grow. Then Heraclês cut off the immortal head, and buried it under a rock; and if it has not been moved, I suppose it is there still. In any case, the marsh is there still, and it still breeds a lot of ugly snakes. The crab was killed too, and actually became a constellation in the sky, but I really cannot see why. From this a proverb grew up in Greece:

> Even Heraclês is done,
> In a fight of two to one.

Heraclês kept the bile of the serpent to dip his arrows in, and thus a wound from his arrows brought death with it.

(3) The Third Labour was the Arcadian Deer. This was a doe, but nevertheless she had antlers,

golden antlers and brazen feet, and she wandered all over Arcadia free, for she was sacred to Artemis. Why that was so is another story which I cannot tell you now, for there are so many stories in Greece that there is no end to them. Heraclês chased the doe for a whole year; and we do not know quite how he caught her, for some say it was in a net, and some say he found her asleep. But in the end, catch her he did, and brought her home on his back. On the way, Artemis met him, and wanted to know what he was doing with her doe. She was very angry, but Heraclês said: "I can't help it: Zeus commands me to obey Eurystheus, and Eurystheus commands me to bring him this doe. So what can I do?" Thus he managed to make peace with Artemis, and brought the doe to his tyrannical master.

(4) The Fourth Labour was the Erymanthian Boar. Like the Lion and the Hydra, this boar was a nuisance to the countryside, where it destroyed cattle and crops, and attacked the people who lived there. Eurystheus told him this time, that he must bring in the boar alive; which seems to be just spiteful, since Heraclês had done the other tasks so well. He had to be careful, you see, not to use too much strength, or too little; for if he used too much, he would kill the boar, and if he used too little, the boar might kill him, or at least damage him.

He set out then, and on his way he passed through the country of the Centaurs. These were monsters, you remember, half horse and half man; they had a man's head and shoulders, and a horse's body; some were a whole man, legs and all, with half a horse growing out behind. They were as swift as a horse, and as strong as a wild beast, and as wise as men. One of them, named Pholos, had a cask of wine; and he said, when he saw Heraclês: "Come into my cave, sir, and let me entertain you; I have a fine drink here which I have been keeping specially for your visit." Heraclês thanked him, and came in; Pholos set cooked meat before him, but he ate his own meat raw.

Then the cask was opened. The wine was a hundred years old. It was indeed a delicious drink, which Heraclês had never tasted before; and it spread abroad such a delicious scent, that the neighbourhood became full of it, and the other Centaurs smelt it, and galloped up to Pholos's cave, to see what it was. When they saw what it was, they crowded into the cave, and began to drink it, which made them wilder than ever.

Now Pholos was frightened, and ran to hide himself, leaving Heraclês to face the furious monsters. They tore up trees by the roots to attack him, and threw great stones at him, and some even picked up axes to cut him down, or drove at him with fire-brands. Their mother, the Cloud, helped them by pouring about them a thick mist, which did little hindrance to the beasts with four legs, but made it difficult not to slip for Heraclês with only two. Yet he was a match for them; he did not even need help this time, and so perhaps he had learnt some-

thing from his fight with the Hydra. He killed a
large number, and the rest he drove away. Among
the killed Centaurs were Horsey and Hilley and Black-
mane, Hit-for-hit, Thumper, and Bristler. Pholos
came back when the fight was over, and looking at
the dead bodies, he pulled out one of the arrows.
"How strange," he said, "that a little thing like that
could kill such great creatures!" and he dropped it
down on the ground; but in dropping, the point
scratched his foot, and as the arrow was poisoned,
Pholos died too.

After this, Heraclês went on in search of the boar;
and he chased him about in the snow, until the boar
fell exhausted in a thicket. Then Heraclês heaved
the boar up on his shoulders, and carried it back to
Eurystheus. He marched into the hall, where
Eurystheus was sitting, and made as though to throw
down the boar at his feet; but Eurystheus, who was
a coward himself, became terrified at the sight, and
ran away, until he saw a large wine-jar buried in the
ground with the neck open; into this jar he jumped
to hide himself. The boar did no mischief to Eurystheus, but Eurystheus went on to find more labours
for Heraclês.

(5) The Fifth Labour was to clean the stables of
Augeas. This Augeas was King of Elis: he had
thirty thousand cattle, and their stables had not been
cleaned for thirty years; but Heraclês was commanded
to clean them in one day. He offered to clean
them out if Augeas would give him one-tenth of
the cattle, and Augeas agreed. Then Heraclês made

gaps in the walls of the stables, one at each end, and turned the course of two rivers towards the upper end; the water ran in at the upper end, and ran out at the lower end, carrying all the dirt with it.   Augeas, however, made an excuse to avoid paying what he had promised. Heraclês punished King Augeas afterwards, for he killed him, and carried off the spoil of the country; and with this spoil he founded the great games at Olympia.

(6) The Sixth Labour was to destroy the Stymphalian Birds. These birds had brazen claws, and brazen wings, and brazen beaks; they used to shoot out their brazen feathers like arrows, and kill people with them, and then they ate their bodies. The birds were gathered about Lake Stymphalos in Arcadia; thence they flew out in swarms, and settled on the fields, and devoured all the crops. Heraclês saw that he could not kill all these birds; but Athena came to his help, and gave him a huge rattle of brass. Heraclês rattled and made a great noise, and the birds rose up; he shot his arrows, and killed some, and the rest flew away. What became of most of them I do not know, but we heard of some of them a little while ago. At least the Stymphalian Lake and the land of Arcadia were quite cleared.

(7) The Seventh Labour was the Cretan Bull. This was a wonderful and beautiful bull, belonging to King Minos of Crete, which had gone mad. Heraclês caught this bull, and carried him on his shoulders to King Eurystheus; then he let the bull loose again, and the bull wandered all over Greece,

and did damage everywhere, until he came to Marathon; and at Marathon he remained.

(8) The Eighth Labour was to capture the Mares of Diomêdês. This man was a savage king of Thrace; he kept his mares fastened with iron chains to mangers of brass, and he used to feed them with the flesh of men. Heraclês called for volunteers to help him; and they went to Thrace and attacked Diomêdês, and gave him to his own mares to eat. The mares then became quiet and tame, and Heraclês easily brought them to Eurystheus.

(9) The Ninth Labour was the Girdle of the Queen of the Amazons. The Amazons were a tribe of women, who fought on horseback like men; and their Queen Hippolyte had a splendid girdle. Heraclês led another body of volunteers against these. When he came to their country, which was in Asia Minor, he demanded the girdle, and Hippolyte came to him quite ready to give it; but the other Amazons thought their queen was being made prisoner, so they attacked Heraclês and his companions. There was a battle, and the Amazons were defeated, and Heraclês brought the girdle back.

(10) The Tenth Labour was the Oxen of Geryonês. This was a horrid monster with three bodies joined at the waist, who lived in an island off the coast of Spain. His oxen were guarded by another monster, and by a dog with two heads. This was a tremendous journey for Heraclês; you see he had been to the far east, and to the north, and now he went to the west,

traversing the north part of Africa. Wherever he went, he cleared the country of wild beasts and serpents, and punished lawless men; for as you remember from the story of his youth, all his life was given to the service of mankind, and he did all his great works without payment.

When he came to the Straits of Gibraltar, he set up two pillars, one on each side, to mark the extreme limit of travel; for the sea and the countries outside the straits were unknown in these early days. These were called ever afterwards, the Pillars of Heraclês.

He then attacked the two-headed dog, and killed it with his club; after which he killed the guardian monster, and shot the three-bodied monster Geryonês with his arrows, and drove the cattle back by land, clearing out the wild beasts on his way, and settling the people in orderly government.

(11) The Eleventh Labour was to fetch the Golden Apples of the Hesperidês. This task was more difficult than usual, because he did not know where they were. So he hunted for them all over the world, and in the course of his journey he had many adventures; amongst them he came to the place where Prometheus was nailed to the rock. Heraclês was angry at the fate of Prometheus; so he set him free, and persuaded Zeus to be kind to him again, and to receive him into the company of Olympos. Prometheus advised Heraclês to find Atlas, his brother, and to ask him where the apples were. For Atlas was the father of the maidens called the Hesperidês,

and they had a garden in the far west, in Spain, where they guarded the golden apples with the help of a dragon.

You remember old Atlas, the Titan, who bore up the heavens upon his shoulders. Heraclês accordingly sought him out, and asked him kindly to show the way to the Garden of the Hesperidês, that he might get the golden apples. Atlas said: "I must not do that, but I will tell you what I will do: I will fetch the apples for you, if you will just hold up the heavens a bit. But I do not think you are strong enough for that." "Not strong enough!" said Heraclês, "I will soon show you." So he stood by Atlas, and Atlas carefully shifted the weight of the heavens upon his head, and Heraclês held it up with his hands.

It was terribly heavy, much worse than he expected; some of the stars fell out as he held it, because he was new to the job, and very glad he was when he saw Atlas coming back. "Here you are," said Atlas, showing him the apples. "What do you want them for?" Heraclês said: "To give to Eurystheus." Then Atlas said: "I can do that, it is no trouble at all," and began to go off. You see, he thought it a great piece of luck that some one had come to relieve him of his job. And Heraclês saw that he was in for it, if he was not careful. No doubt his talk with Prometheus had sharpened his wits, for he did not show anger or apprehension, whatever he felt; but all he said was: "I thank you, I am much obliged, but just give me a little help first. I am not used to this weight, and it is rather uncomfortable; hold it a minute while I make a pad for my head." Atlas was not clever, like his brother Prometheus, who had all the brains of the family; he was a stupid thing like his uncle Cronos: so he agreed at once, and laid the apples down on the ground. Then Heraclês thanked him, and shifted the heavens upon Atlas's shoulders again, and picked up the apples, and went off to Eurystheus. I do not know what Atlas said. The heaven has not fallen down yet, so we may suppose the old Titan still does his duty: but we shall see.

(12) The Last Labour was to fetch up the dog Cerberos from Tartaros. There is a dark cave in Mount Tainaron, which is the entrance to Tartaros, and a dark tunnel downwards; and by this way Heraclês went down. He had some adventures in the lower world which you will hear of later; and Hadês allowed him to take Cerberos, if he could do so without using his weapons. Heraclês therefore seized the dog with his hands, and crushed him tight until his spirit was tamed; then he carried him up into the world, and showed him to Eurystheus, after which he brought him back to remain as the watch-dog of Hadês.

And so you see Heraclês led the life he had chosen when he was a young man; and these years of penance under Eurystheus he spent in exploring the world, and clearing it of dangerous monsters, and making it better for men to live in. I have not told you half his great deeds yet; many of them come in amongst his Labours, but it is convenient to keep the Twelve Labours together.

One of these deeds was the battle with the Giants. Zeus had already got rid of most of the ancient monsters, but a troop of giants remained, and to conquer these the oracle declared it necessary to seek the help of a mortal. Heraclês therefore was summoned to help; and the battle was joined on the plain of Phlegra.

The Giants, like other such, used huge rocks and trees to throw at their enemies, and burning firebrands. One of them split off a chunk of the island Cos, and threw it at his enemy; you may see to-day how large it was, for it fell in the sea, and is now called the island of Nisyros. Another of them, Alcyoneus, whenever he was knocked down, jumped up again stronger than ever. For it was fated that he could not be killed upon the land where he was born. So the goddess Athena, who had plenty of sense, told Heraclês to drag him over the boundary of his land, into the next; and there they killed him easily enough. Zeus struck some with his thunderbolt; Athena and Poseidon, Apollo and Artemis, all took part, and Heraclês was not wanting. The Giants were destroyed, and their bodies were buried under volcanoes, and islands in the sea. So now we see gods and men on the same side. Men were becoming better, and Zeus was more friendly towards them, for there was no more talk of destroying mankind. And in fact, gods and men are now so mixed up that it is impossible to tell of them separately.

Madness came upon Heraclês once more, which led to a strange adventure. In his madness he killed a friend without knowing what he did. When he recovered his senses, he went to the oracle of Apollo, at Delphi, to ask what he should do, in order to be made pure from this deed of bloodshed; but the priestess would give him no answer. This made him angry, and he said: "Very well, I will make an oracle of my own!" Then he seized Apollo's tripod, where the priestess used to sit, and began to carry it off. As he went off, who should meet him at the door of the temple but Apollo himself! Apollo took hold of one leg, Heraclês held to the others, and there was a great fight between them, Heraclês pulling one way, and Apollo the other. I do not know which would have won; but while they were pulling away, Zeus came between them. He said: "What is the meaning of this? No fighting in the family, please; you will only break the thing, if you pull it like that." Then he dropped a little speck of a thunderbolt between them which fizzled up and startled them both. "Now," he said, "put it back; and give Heraclês his answer."

So Heraclês got his answer, and the answer was this: he was to be sold as a slave, and to work for three years, and then he was to pay the price paid for him to the soul of the man he had killed.

So Hermês sold him, and he was bought by Omphalê, queen of Lydia, and she set him many tasks to do. Some of them were worthy of Heraclês, for she made him clear out the robbers and brigands from her country. One of these was named the Stripper. He used to catch wayfarers, and rob them, and make them dig about his vines with a spade; Heraclês knocked him on the head with his own spade.

There were also two brothers, full of mischief, who used to creep into the houses and steal. They must have been like a pair of ugly monkeys, for they were named Cerkôpês, which means Tailyboys. Their mother knew about their doings, but all she did was to give them a warning: "Ware Heraclês!"

Then one day Heraclês caught them. He trussed them up like a pair of fowls, and hung them head downwards on the two ends of a pole, and then he set off, carrying the pole across his shoulders, like a milkman. The boys were quite cheerful, and did nothing but crack jokes. "Who are you, pray?" they asked. He said: "I am Heraclês." As they were hanging head downwards, they had a good view of his legs, which were all covered with black hair; and one said: "You call yourself Hairyclês, do you? I call you Hairy-knees!" This pleased Heraclês, who liked a joke himself; so he let them off easily. Omphalê also liked a joke; so she used to make Heraclês put on her dress, and she put on his lion-skin, and then she gave him a distaff and spindle, and made him spin wool into thread. When the three years were up, he paid the fine, and he was now held to be free from guilt.

Heraclês also joined the quest of the Golden Fleece,

a great adventure, which we heard of in the story of the Argonauts. He also once met Theseus, a great hero like himself, and he had many other adventures which I must pass over; but there is one that I must tell, because that is the beginning of the story of Troy.

It begins in the early days of the reign of Zeus, when he had troubles without and troubles within. Only a hint has come down in memory; we only know that there was a conspiracy of the gods against Zeus. A party of them wanted to dethrone him, and put him in prison; and in this party was his wife Hera, and his daughter Athena, with his brother Poseidon, and his son Apollo. That might have been the end of Zeus, but for the sea-nymph Thetis, who was afterwards mother of Achillês. Thetis had a happy thought; why not call in the help of the hundred-handed monster, Briareos? And so he did: Briareos came to help his old friend, who had set him free once upon a time. You may imagine how it amazed the gods, plotting together in the corner, when they saw the monster march in, full of pride and power, waving his hundred hands about, and saw him sit down by the side of Zeus! Zeus punished Apollo and Poseidon, by sending them down to earth, and commanding them to serve the King of Troy for wages, one year long. They had to build the walls of Troy, and hard work it was, as Poseidon said afterwards; but when the year was up, and they asked for their wages, the King gave them none; he only said: "Get out, or I will cut off

And then he set off, carrying the pole across his shoulders, like a milkman.

both your ears, and sell you to be slaves in the islands!"

I suppose he did not know who they were, but he soon found out, when they became gods again. For Apollo sent a pestilence, and Poseidon sent a sea-monster, who caught the people and swallowed them up. This went on until the King enquired of an oracle, which told him that he would be free if he gave his daughter to the monster. Accordingly he left his daughter on the sea-shore, securely tied, for the monster to eat. But he asked Heraclês to deliver her, and promised that if he did, he would give as a reward his precious mares to Heraclês: for he had some wonderful mares of a divine breed. Then Heraclês attacked the monster. It was a terrible monster; Heraclês leapt into its mouth, and went down into its belly; there he was three days and nights, cutting and hacking, until he cut his way out, and made an end of it at last.

So Heracles killed the monster, and delivered the maiden. He told her that she was free to go home, unless she would rather come away with him; she said she would rather come with him, for fear another monster might come along later. But the King refused to give either his daughter or the mares: he was as bad as ever, you see. Then Heraclês went away, and soon came back with a fleet; they besieged Troy, and broke through the wall, and stormed the city. The King was killed, and Heraclês made one of his sons king in his place. This man was called

King Priam, who comes in Homer's story of the great Trojan War.

We are now coming to the last scene in the life of Heraclês. His home now was in Calydon, a district in North Greece, not far from the place where the English poet, Lord Byron, died, in 1824, helping to make the Greeks free. The King of Calydon had a beautiful daughter, named Deïaneira, and she was wooed by the god of the great river Acheloös, which runs through the country. The wooer was rather alarming; for he appeared first in the form of a bull, then in the form of a serpent with shining coils, then like a man with a bull's head. You may imagine that Deïaneira was pleased when a proper man appeared, that is Heraclês himself. There was a great fight between Heraclês and the bull, but Heraclês won; and the maiden became his wife. But she lived in great anxiety, because Heraclês had to go away upon so many adventures; and she was a little jealous too, for fear he should fall in love with some one else, on his travels.

It happened that they had to travel away from Calydon together; and on the way, there was a river to cross. At the crossing, there was a Centaur, half man and half horse, named Nessos, who used to ferry travellers over the river. Heraclês told Nessos to carry over his wife; but when Nessos was across on the bank, he laid hold of her, and began to carry her off. Heraclês saw this from the other side, and at once shot an arrow, which struck the death-blow of Nessos.

But Nessos was an evil creature; and guessing that Deïaneira might be jealous, he said to her: "Now I am about to die, I wish to make up to you for my evil attempt. Catch some of my blood as it drops from the wound, and it shall be a charm for you; if your husband ever ceases to love you, this charm will win back his love. Keep it carefully away from the sun, and far from the fire, and when you want to use it, put it like ointment upon him." She caught the blood in a jar, and the Centaur died; and she kept this blood secretly, with great care, sealed up in the jar, away from fire and sunlight.

Now when Heraclês was coming back from one of his adventures, victorious as usual, and with a long train of captives, she found out that one of the captives was a very beautiful maiden, and they said that Heraclês was in love with her. So Deïaneira took out her jar, and poured the blood upon the inside of a long robe, which she had woven herself, and sent it to her husband by a messenger. The robe was folded up, and laid in a box to carry; she told the messenger to give it to her husband, that he might wear it when he did sacrifice in thanksgiving for a safe return.

But when the messenger was gone, she was terribly frightened. As she was spreading the stuff upon the robe, a drop had fallen upon a piece of wool that lay near, and when the robe was gone, she happened to look at the wool, and saw that it was smouldering—then it broke into a flame, and all shrivelled up into ashes. She waited in great anxiety until the messenger should return; and there was good reason for it, for by and by the messenger did return, and she heard an awful story.

Heraclês took the robe, and put it on, and began his sacrifice. But the sunlight worked on the stuff through the robe, and he felt first a tickling, then a burning; the robe clung close to his limbs, and by degrees burnt into his flesh; they laid him down on a couch, and in a short time he perished. But his soul went to heaven, and there dwelt among the gods. They gave him a house to live in, and a heavenly bride, Hêbê the goddess of youth; as if to say that Heraclês, after all his troubles, was to live for ever young and strong as he was in his youth. So the prophecy was fulfilled that he heard in his young days. He lived a noble life, he had many troubles, and in the end he gained fame and immortality.

XI

CASTOR AND POLYDEUCES

CASTOR and his brother, Polydeuces, or Pollux as the Romans called him, had a wonderful fate.

Men were always running about in those days, and lifting their neighbours' cattle, like the English and Scotch raiders on the borders long ago. So at one time, Castor and his brother joined Idas and Lynceus in a raid: Idas was the strong man, you remember, and Lynceus had sharp eyes, and could see anything on earth and under the earth. They drove off a lot of cattle from Arcadia, and then they sat down to divide the spoil.

"Look here," said Idas, "I'll divide it, and this is my way. I will cut up this cow into four parts," and this he did. "Now then, let us have an eating match. Whoever eats his part first shall have half the spoil, and whoever eats his part second shall have the other half."

They agreed, but before they knew where they were, Idas had swallowed his own share and then his brother's, and they drove off the cattle together.

This did not suit the others at all; so they gave chase to the town where Idas and Lynceus were, and drove off the cattle and a lot of others besides, and lay in wait for Idas and Lynceus.

As they gave chase in their turn, Lynceus cried out:

"Hullo! I spy Castor! Hit him Idas! There he is crouching under the stump of an oak!"

So they ran up to the spot. Idas thrust a spear into Castor and left him gasping; then Polydeuces came after them, and they stood beside a great tomb-stone which was there on the mountain. They pulled up the pillar between them, and thrust it at Polydeuces, but the blow did not shake him, and he rushed at Lynceus and drove his blade into his side. Zeus struck down Idas with a thunderbolt, for Castor and Polydeuces were his own sons.

Polydeuces returned to his brother, and found him dying on the ground. Then he cried out to Zeus:

"Father, what is to be the end of our sorrows? Let me die with him!"

Zeus came to him, and cried:

"My son, I will take you up to heaven and make you immortal. But if you love your brother so much, and if you wish to give him an equal share of everything, you may share immortality between you. Half your time you shall be under the earth, and half in heaven, and so with him also."

The young man agreed at once, and so it was: they had one day each on earth, and one each in heaven.

But they did not see much of each other so; and in later days Poseidon allowed them to have power over winds and waves, and to protect travellers by sea; and they were worshipt all over the land as the Saviour Gods. Mariners thought they were in the St. Elmo's fire, which perches on the mast sometimes in stormy weather, and they especially revered these gods.

XII

AMPHIARAOS

THE seer, Amphiaraos, had a sadder fate.

He was both seer and warrior, and his wife was Eriphyle, the daughter of Adrastos, King of Argos. This King became mixt up in the quarrel about Thebes, which you may know from the story of Oedipus; his two sons, whose names I need not trouble you with, had quarrelled as to which ought to be King, and they agreed at last to take a year each. Then the younger, after his year was done, said he was not going to turn out now; and the elder escaped to Argos, and there he married another daughter of King Adrastos. He was so angry with his brother and so hot with the King, that he persuaded the King to lead a large army against Thebes, commanded by the Seven Champions.

But Amphiaraos knew that the army was to fail, by decree of Fate, and he refused to go. What was the young Theban prince to do? He thought of something.

At the wedding of Cadmos and Harmonia, the gods were present, and one of the gods gave Harmonia a wonderful necklace, which afterwards brought bad luck to everyone who had it.

Harmonia had four daughters, who each received the necklace in turn. One daughter was Semele who became the wife of Zeus. She was so greedy that she wished to see Zeus in all his pomp and glory, and when he so appeared, the thunder struck her and the lightning burnt her up. Another was Ino, whose husband went mad, and chased her into the sea. Another was Autonoe, whose son was changed into a stag, and his own hounds tore him to pieces. The fourth was Agauë, who went mad herself, and thought her son was a wild beast, and killed him and cut off his head.

This necklace the young Theban promised to Eriphyle, if she would persuade her husband to join in the expedition to Thebes. You might expect that she would have taken care to keep clear of that necklace, but not a bit of it! Give her the necklace, and Argos and her father and her husband might all go hang. So she persuaded her husband to support the King's wish, and he did so, although he knew that the result would be ruin; and so it was, and no one came back from that expedition except Adrastos. All the champions perished, and the two royal brothers killed one another.

But Amphiaraos did not die on the field; he fled away, and as he went the earth swallowed him up with his chariot and horses. Adrastos mourned him, and said: "I miss the eye of my army, both a good seer and a warrior excellent in battle."

XIII

ORPHEUS

LASTLY we come to the minstrel, Orpheus.

To the sound of his harp, the ship Argo glided down into the sea. The sound of his harp made the Clashing Rocks stand still just one minute, when the Argo was passing through. The sound of his harp helped to send the sleepless dragon to sleep.

You see he was a rare hand with the harp; and no wonder, for his father was Apollo, and Apollo taught him to play upon his own harp. He played so beautifully, that all the wild beasts on Mount Olympos used to come and lie down all around him, to listen. More than that, even the trees would pluck up their roots, if they were not too old and too deep, and hop along to listen. Even the rocks rolled out of their places, and came to listen. All the country people were enchanted; the wild Satyrs used to dance round him, wagging their tails.

He married a wife named Eurydicê, whom he loved very much. One day Eurydicê trod on a snake, which bit her foot, and she died.

Orpheus would not be comforted. He played on his harp no more; he wandered over the mountains, and through the forests, and mourned his lost wife. At last he determined that he would go down to the dark house of Hadês, and bring her back.

So he entered the dark cave, and traversed the dark tunnel which led through the earth, to the dark house of Hadês. When he came to the gate, the three-headed dog Cerberos growled, and would have bitten him; but Orpheus played a soft tune on his harp, and the dog dropped his three heads on his paws, and gently wagged his tail, and let Orpheus go by.

When he came to the great hall of Hadês, what a sight met his eyes! There sat King Hadês and Queen Persephonê, on their thrones. There sat the three Judges of the Dead, Minos, Rhadamanthys and Aiacos—for there is justice in the house of Hadês. Every soul, when it comes into that place, must give account for deeds done in the body: those who are good are dismissed to the Elysian Fields, to be at peace; those who are bad receive punishment proper to their deeds.

There Orpheus saw some of the great sinners enduring their punishment. He saw a family of nine-and-forty sisters, the Danaïds, who had all been married on one day, and had murdered their husbands in the night. They were condemned to draw water, and carry it to a huge vessel in jars with holes in the bottom, so as fast as they poured the water in, it ran out.

He saw the punishment of the cruel King Tantalos. In his life on earth, Tantalos once entertained the gods at a feast. Like the wicked King of Arcadia, he wanted to see if they really had more wisdom than men. So he killed his own son Pelops, and cooked the body, and offered it to the gods to eat. They all knew it at once, and refused, except Demeter, who ate a bit of the shoulder, because she had just lost her daughter and did not know what she was doing. Pelops was brought back to life, and made well again, all but the bit of his shoulder, which was a-missing: but Demeter put an ivory shoulder in its place. This Tantalos was punished by being hungry and thirsty for ever. He stood in the middle of a lake of water: when he bent down his head to drink, the water all slid away; if he scooped up a handful, the water ran through his fingers. All round the water grew trees laden with fruit, apples and pears, figs, and grapes, and oranges; when he stretched out his hand to pluck one, the tree whisked it away into the air above him. Did your father ever call you a tantalizing brat? If so, he was re-minding you of Tantalos, who was always dis-appointed when he hoped for something good.

He saw Sisyphos, the most cunning and deceitful of men, who had betrayed the secrets of the gods. His punishment was to roll a huge stone up to the top of a hill: he pushed with head and shoulders, panting and sweating and covered with dust; but whenever he got to the top, the stone would gently slide off on one side or the other, and roll down to the bottom. Then he had to begin all over again.

He saw Ixion, who also had committed an act of

When he came to the gate, the three-headed dog Cerberos growled.

treachery to the gods. His punishment was the strangest of all. He was fastened to a wheel with four spokes, one for each leg and arm, and the wheel went round and round for ever.

That was the scene which met the eye of Orpheus, as he entered the dark house of Hadês. The soul of Eurydicê was there waiting, for her case had not yet been heard; there were so many waiting for judgment. But Orpheus pleaded with Hadês, that he might take her back to life.

Hadês said: "Why should I treat her otherwise than I treat the other souls?"

Orpheus was silent: then his eyes flashed, and he said, in a loud voice: "This is why!" and struck up a tune on his harp. The melody began soft, then rose, and rang loudly through the dark hall: and as the melody sounded, Hadês leaned forward on his throne and listened, Persephonê turned her head and sat still and listened, the three judges ceased their questions and listened, the Danaïds stood still and listened, and let the water do what it would, the water ceased to run out of the holes, Tantalos's lake stood still and Tantalos had a good drink, then he listened too, the stone of Sisyphos rolled up to Orpheus and lay still, Ixion's wheel stood still and Ixion with it, to listen to the wonderful sounds. At last Hadês said: "Your music is worth a life. Take her and go: but be very careful never to look back at her till you come to your own door."

Orpheus was glad enough to have her on any conditions; so he turned round, and went towards the gate, still playing upon his harp, and Eurydicê followed him. Out of the gate he went, still playing, past the three-headed Cerberos, along the dark tunnel, out of the dark cave, and then he thought to himself, "I wonder if Eurydicê is following," for he could not hear her footsteps. Without thinking, he turned to look: there she was, close behind—but even as he looked, she uttered a cry, she began to fade, and in a few moments, like a wisp of smoke, she had vanished.

Now there was no hope for Orpheus. But he seems to have learnt the wisdom of the gods by his journey to the house of Hadês; for he no longer played on his harp, but he made wonderful poems, telling mankind what to do if they wished to please the gods, and to be happy after death. Some say he also taught them to eat only vegetables, and not to kill animals for food. Perhaps he remembered how sensible the animals were in listening to his music; but that can hardly be the reason, for the trees listened too, and no doubt the vegetables would have listened if they had been handy.

But Orpheus would not marry another wife. There were a number of wild women in Thrace, where he lived, and they used to hold feasts in honour of Dionysos every year, and madden themselves with wine. Some say they were angry because Orpheus would not take one of them to wife: whatever the reason may be, these women set on him and killed him, and cut off his head, and threw it into the river Hebros. The river carried it into the sea, and it floated across to the island of Lesbos, by the town of Methymna, where it was washed ashore. And ever since that time, right down to our own day, the nightingales in the olive trees round Methymna sing more sweetly than any other nightingales in the world.

www.ingramcontent.com/pod-product-compliance
Lightning Source LLC
Chambersburg PA
CBHW021735190726
48288CB00009B/3052